Praise for

The *Girlfriend* Manifesto

"Ms. Ashmore writes with the tone of that girlfriend we have known for years, as her story is relatable to its core. It's a breezy read and you'll find yourself reflecting on ideas, long after you have put it down." **Brooke Holder** (Mississippi, US)

"It's an incredibly engaging read ~ Susie's innovative style with short snippets and email format made it easy to digest and quick to get into. Susie not only provides some good entertainment, but also has great motivational messages with insight for all."
Jody Ridpath (Toronto, Canada)

"From a guy's perspective, the title of this book may seem like a penned chick-flick, but the content is universal. It was an easy read and I was riveted, wondering the outcome of each adventure. At some point in life, many of us go through these waters. This story will cause you to reminisce and inspire you to start your own journey." **Scott S.** (Halifax, Canada)

"Fantastic! It had me hooked from beginning to end. Susie gives you a front row seat to her story and will have you simply unable to put this book down." **Stacia Doan** (Washington State, US)

"Loved it! A humorous and engaging account of living, loving and, at times, unravelling the complexities of relationships that anyone could relate to." **Jennifer Nicholas** (Perth, Australia)

THE *Girlfriend* MANIFESTO

Susie Ashmore

E-mails appear courtesy of the original authors.
Names and identifying details have been changed accordingly.
The questions from the workshop Getting Your Life on a Roll appear courtesy of Wayne Vanwyck,
CEO of The Achievement Centre International.
Clip art is used with permission from Microsoft.
Regina Brett appears courtesy of Cleveland's The Plain Dealer.

Revised Edition ~ May 2025

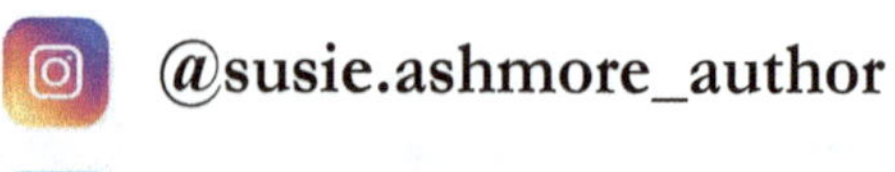
@susie.ashmore_author

susie.ashmore@rogers.com

To J.,
the spark that lit the flame of this entire journey

To my Cupids and Bachelors,
the heart and soul of the story within

To A.,
the gold standard for living life to the fullest

And finally...to my parents,
who have always told me to do what I love,
hence, the courage that blossomed
and the adventures that have unfolded

The new app, 5 Dates Plan, is now available.

To **set up** & **track** your own **5 Dates**,

visit

The App Store

or

@susie.ashmore_author

If your ship doesn't come in,

swim out to meet it.

Jonathan Winters

Table of Contents

Words of Wisdom

From: Vivienne
To: Sophie
Subject: **Your blessings**
Date: Wednesday, April 26 8:57 pm

Dear Sophie,

I wish I were closer so I could grab on tight and not let go.

Please remember to stop and count your blessings. You are surrounded by *so much* love and support. You have a wonderful little boy who loves you, who needs you and who wants you to be happy. Just let go. Let go and have faith that the world will right itself. In a relationship, you need to *know* what to expect from your partner, not *worry* about what to expect. You must be each other's soft place to fall; each other's safe place. If that is not what you have, then let go, Sophie. Let go with love. Let go with faith.

I love you, Sophie, and I want you to know that you deserve to have a happy, relaxed life...and a happy, relaxed relationship. You need that and deserve that, and so does your little boy.

Please call any time.
Vivienne xo

The Right Thing

My relationship was far too complex for words to capture with any remote chance of accuracy. He was the ultimate man of my dreams, but laced with complications I just couldn't untangle, no matter how hard I tried. Staying with him was not an option; yet leaving him proved to be pathetically unsuccessful, over and over and over again.

Mistake # 1 – On our first date, listening to him admit to insurance fraud in a very nonchalant way, then ignoring the raised hairs on the back of my neck while he confessed with a complete lack of remorse. I always thought that it was just an expression. But those fine little hairs that you can barely see back there? They really do stand straight up. Like a highly trained soldier. It is your body telling you, **I can't explain this in 3 seconds or less, but you need to turn around and run like hell.** Which we never do. And by we, I mean women. We likely have the strongest instincts on the planet, yet for some unknown reason, we seem to trust ourselves the least in this world. It really is like having your very best friend propped up high on your left shoulder, looking out for you from every angle. And why wouldn't we trust our very best friend? We need a mandatory course in high school that teaches us all to recognize all those little warning signs and interpret them as a freight train coming at us at full speed ahead, with horns and whistles blaring...piercing our every awareness.

But he was everything I wanted. Everything I had *always* wanted. On paper, that is. Smart, funny, successful, athletic. Attractive with a body that was a clone of Michelangelo's Statue of David. And nice. He was *incredibly* nice. How could one little comment make me throw it all away?

In addition to him seeming to meet my every criteria for a mate, let's face it: I was desperate. I had finally stumbled across my tropical oasis after a very long, very dry trek across the hot desert sands. And man, was I thirsty. Single men were rare ~ practically unheard of in our sleepy little town. Dating was hard enough for anyone, but being a single mom made it all that much more challenging. But, finally...FINALLY! Here was a great guy from my ski club who was interesting…and interested. And, available. Officially available. I was tired of getting hit on by married men ~ a novelty that wears off pretty quickly, I'd say. A lawyer while we were on vacation in Tobago; his wife and son within full view. A cop who interviewed me repeatedly as a witness to a white-collar crime.

The list goes on. I called my girlfriend, Julia, one night to share my shocking news with her that I had just been hit on by a good friend's husband. **Whose???** she teased, trying not to wake Grace, asleep in her arms. **Because if it's mine, as long as Tim is home by 8 am, I'm fine with it!**

Mistake # 2 – Laughing it off when he said, early on, in his creamy, dreamy telephone voice, that someone had told him that he had a split personality and that he shouldn't date women. Now, come on. How could I not see that as a *massive* red flag ~ a sign to drop everything and head for the hills? But he said it in such a funny, charming way. I honestly thought it was just self-deprecating humour.

These two mistakes - these two teeny, tiny mistakes - turned out to be, without a doubt, the biggest ones of my life.

And so, here I was, so deeply attached...so deeply unable to un-attach myself from him and his tangled web…so addicted to his wonderful and charismatic side, that I had to send myself text messages to survive this much-needed break-up ~ to stay away for good this time:

April 25

9:57 am **You are doing the right thing**

9:57 am **Enough is enough**

9:58 am **Things will never change**

10:31 am It's time to move on

10:38 am You deserve a better life

10:39 am Today will be a good one

10:40 am You can do this

April 26

6:31 am Be strong

6:32 am Love yourself enough to do this

6:32 am Love Cameron enough to do this

5:36 pm Blue skies ahead

5:36 pm See the rainbow after the storm

But, as predictable as the rising sun, I allowed myself to fall right back into his arms…exactly how I said I would never do. I'd literally lost count of the number of feeble attempts I'd made to free my mind and soul from this very broken relationship. Accepting his request for forgiveness, yet again, was tangible proof that my ability to detox him from my veins was hopelessly impossible. This continuous failure to release myself made no sense for a woman like me. Confident, successful, happy in life...happy with myself. It just didn't add up. I was pure confirmation that there is not an ounce of room in a bleeding heart for common sense or inner strength.

My weekly routine had become not only chronic, but unbearably monotonous, as well. Every Monday morning, I would stand at the front of my class of 8-year-old girls, glaring up at me with such pure innocence, and know that what I had just endured with his depression over the weekend would never be good enough for any one of them. And I would even apply it to myself, realizing that what I had just endured was not good enough for me, either, on a truly enormous scale.

It was not the breaking free part that I couldn't do. It was the staying free part that I simply could not sustain. I once said to my therapist that, if she were the marriage police and I asked her permission to marry him, I knew that she would have to deny my request. I even realized that, if a girlfriend of mine was staying in a relationship like this, I would a) have no clue whatsoever as to why; and b) demand up and down that she leave the him immediately and head straight to Bali with her favourite girlfriends.

So, I knew. I was fully capable of separating myself from the situation to appreciate the vital importance of leaving him. But, just not capable of keeping him away. Beyond all logic, I kept allowing him to crawl back into my life, despite my exhaustive efforts to stay strong...foolishly believing his every promise to seek medical assistance, once and for all.

I tell you ~ this thing called love is an entity, all of its own. When we are addicted to alcohol, drugs, gambling...we betray our loved ones. But, when we are addicted to love, we betray ourselves. I was living, walking, breathing proof of it.

Bottom line: love shouldn't be this hard. You shouldn't have to go to the ends of the earth within a relationship, especially when they refuse treatment. I wish someone had shouted that through a megaphone, to make me wake up out of this nightmare, once and for all. Time heals most things that are worth saving. This relationship was definitely not worth saving.

4 Months Later...
Searching for Rainbows

From: Sophie
To: Vivienne
Subject: Searching for Rainbows
Sent: Tuesday, September 5 10:39 pm

Hi there, Sweets...

I've been wanting to call you the last few days - including tonight, but look at the time. And my day has finally just ended. How are you? I was thinking that the chicken store would have been crazy busy for you today with it being the first day back at school for everyone. You must be exhausted. We almost got take-out tonight ourselves, but luckily my mom gave us one of her famous home-cooked meals instead.

I am happy to say that I had a good first day - my class is so much better than last year ~ by a mile, thank god. (I don't know their skills yet, but who cares! They are well behaved!)

Cameron had a good day as well but he said that it was a bit tough having to convert everything into French again, all in one shot. But you know what that is like.

Do you have a minute? I need a serious shoulder to cry on right now, since, well...when it rains, it pours, and there is a hurricane blasting through my world right now. My boss is on a rampage with everyone as per usual and we all spend each day trying to avoid her like the plague. Plus, I have had to end things with Troy - and this is truly, truly the last time, for so many crucial reasons. I am a mess - not eating...not sleeping. On top of all that, I tore my knee again about 2 weeks ago, and my cleaning lady just doubled her prices and now she is charging more per hour than I make. No joke! So, go figure. My life feels like it is falling apart in all directions right now. I know it could be worse – a lot worse - so I shouldn't complain. But I just need to vent.

I feel like I will never find another partner again. Or ever want one again, for that matter. I haven't told anyone, but Troy was diagnosed with severe depression and is refusing treatment of any kind. The worst part is that there is no warning – it just comes out of nowhere, like when I say "How was your day, honey?" And, boom. He goes into complete silence for days. I left him so many times but foolishly kept believing his every promise to get medical help, which always led to a hopeless dead end. Have I told you that I have lost a ton of weight since being with him, without even trying? Not a good sign. There is a commercial on TV that says "Depression hurts everyone", and boy, is that ever true.

Sorry for just pouring everything out like this. This is the hardest time I have ever experienced in my life. I have not actually told Cameron yet, but I'll have to do it this weekend.

Thanks for listening. I'm so lucky to have you in my life. Enough about me. How are the two of you? Let me live vicariously through you! (Please!!!)

Sophie xoxox

From: Vivienne

To: Sophie

Subject: **Re: Searching for Rainbows**

Date: Thursday, September 7   9:13 pm

Hi Sophie,

The good news is definitely your class!! Well behaved? That's worth its weight in gold!

You know, I understand when you write "I feel like I will never find another partner again". That's exactly how I felt 10 years ago, just months before I met Ben. I finally just accepted that it wasn't within my control whether or not I found someone, and I sat down and counted my blessings. I actually remember doing that. I knew that, what would be, would be, and I set out to enjoy what I had.

Sophie, you have so many rainbows in your life. You can stop searching.

I hope you have another great day with the little ones at school tomorrow. I'll call on the weekend.

Much love,

Vivienne

September 8

6:50 am He creates chaos

7:21 am You lost 20 lbs trying to help him

7:22 am You had walk away

7:22 am Celebrate that you are free

The weekend was drawing to a close and I had yet to share any of the news with Cameron. We had had a really great weekend together and I guess I just didn't want to spoil the tranquility of it all. But the weight of the world that was resting on my shoulders was becoming unbearable, as I procrastinated in sharing that Troy would no longer be in our lives. I remember last Christmas, Cameron saying to him that he had 3 more chances. I guess he was literally saying, "Three strikes and you're out." So many women foolishly 'stay in it for the kids', yet they say that kids are actually hugely relieved when a wrong relationship finally ends. So, why was I dreading the inevitable that was about to unfold?

It was bath time, which seems to always bring the very best conversations out of the mouths of babes. Something about a very busy boy finally slowing down long enough for true heart-to-heart conversations to emerge. But instead of words slipping out, it was tears. My tears. One at a time, silently, politely taking turns rolling down my cheeks. I guess, by telling Cameron, it would make it all completely real ~ that it would truly be over, and that I wouldn't be able to keep trying to make things work anymore.

Without missing a beat, Cameron asked, as he casually moved the bubbles up and down the length of the bath, Why are you crying?

I'm not sure, I replied quietly.

Well, you should figure out what is making you cry, and then ask yourself if it is worth crying about.

He was barely a Grade 2 graduate, and yet here he was, playing in the bathtub, somehow able to demonstrate the wisdom and insight of Oprah and Brené Brown combined, as if they were whispering in each ear. And the worst part? Cameron was right. I was crying over a man who was terrible for me. Wonderful at times, yes. But terrible for me inside and out. So terrible, that his medical team insisted that I leave him. But when he was good, he was beautiful and amazing, and that was just so incredibly hard to let go of and walk away from.

From: Debra
To: Sophie
Subject: Our chat
Date: Friday, September 22 8:52 am

Hey Sophie,

Great to see you the other night - as always! I felt afterwards like we went to some pretty deep places and I have been very reflective for the last few days. Thanks for the safe space to just "be", and for being such an authentic and passionate friend.

I am sorry to hear of your break-up. But I know that as you move forward - from relief to reflection to release – you will only deepen the happiness in your life. Keep the faith!

Big hugs and lots of love,

Debra

October 2

9:54 am You can do this

9:55 am You had to do this

10:13 am You had no choice

10:14 am He needs professional help

10:15 am Make it a good day

10:15 am Smile...!

12:10 pm Count your blessings

It was the day after Thanksgiving and the luxuries of a 3-day weekend had come to a screeching halt with the rude awakening of the early morning alarm. I started the day with the usual weekday routine of making breakfast smoothies and school lunches...only to be interrupted by a single yet deafening bark.

It was so out of the ordinary that I went and peaked around the corner, only to my shock of horrors to find Coconut, our little white Maltese, sitting majestically up on top of the dining room table...like he owned the joint.

At last night's festivities, I hosted the turkey dinner with everyone gathered in the dining room for most of the night. With Coconut being just a puppy, it was likely the first time he had seen so much activity focused around the big table like that. I guess he figured that it was time he got in on the action, too. A little 'better late than never', but why not?

I didn't know whether to laugh or be mad. Instead, I grabbed my camera. I had to have proof of this mischievous conduct.

Three minutes later, again. But this time no bark, just nonchalantly sitting on top of the coffee table in the family room – the site of last night's appetizers - practically right under my nose as I was packing lunches. Still not an ounce of guilt or remorse anywhere in sight.

Again, with complete astonishment, I snatched the camera.

Four minutes later. Another bark. This time I recognized the tone and arrived prepared to get yet another unbelievable photo of my sweet-little-angel turned bold-little-devil, up on the dining room table. Again! Seriously???

I couldn't help myself and said out loud to him in disbelief, **I don't get it. You climb up on top of the table like you're King of the Jungle, knowing what you're getting yourself into, and then you deliberately try to get caught.** (Obviously, a reality TV star in the making.)

I was especially thankful to have Coconut in our lives as a much-needed distraction. I had never actually held a dog before due to allergies and so, as a result, I had absolutely no concept as to how they can thunder in, steal your heart and fill it with more love than seems humanly possible.

We had purchased him on Valentine's Day, despite my last words to Cameron before we got out of the car, shaking my finger at him as he sat in the back seat. **Now, remember. We are *NOT* getting a dog. We're a fish family.** But it was literally love at first sight and it was me asking the fateful question, **How much for the little white one?** From there on out, it was game over. I was so smitten that I was willing to ignore Julia's polite but realistic warning on the phone later that night that it would be an irreversible commitment for the next 17 years. It was a true example of intoxicating love. I dove right in as if three-sheets-to-the-wind, like an olive, heavily marinated in a vodka martini. Completely sloshed with infatuation.

Despite this impulsive and seemingly reckless choice, it turned out to be, truly, one of the best decisions I've ever made. It was our adorable puppy who was single-handedly responsible for happiness gushing through our veins ~ much needed, as I continued to struggle with letting go. Emotional turmoil needed to be replaced with delightful goodness. And it just happened to come in the form of a little white fluffball named Coconut.

Despite my happiness, self-help was still in great demand:

October 26

7:23 am You are doing an amazing job

7:23 am Be proud of yourself

October 27

6:54 am You're a superstar

6:55 am Be thankful that you let go

Hallowe'en. The one day of the year with endless distractions. And yet, the nightmare still haunted...

October 31

10:56 am You are strong

10:57 am You've got this

10:57 am Enjoy the peace in your life now

10:58 am Stay strong

10:59 am You will rise above this

11:00 am You had absolutely no choice

November 6

10:21 am Life is good

November 9

9:56 am Remember the other side of him

9:58 am Life is so much better without him

9:58 am Hurray! Life is calm...

November 17

10:32 am A new beginning

10:33 am A bright future awaits

10:34 am Life is divine without him

10:38 am He is not in a healthy place

November 21

10:12 am Look at you!

10:13 am Enjoy the sunshine

10:13 am It's a beautiful day

November 23

10:12 am You're almost there!

November 24

1:15 pm You're doing so well!

November 30

10:00 am Feel better :)

Even with the distractions of the Christmas season...

December 11

10:03 am Feeling good

December 13

7:35 am Today will be fantastic!

December 14

8:39 am Remember how hard it was

Four months since I broke up with him and I was still coaching myself. But the tides had turned.

January 8

10:10 am You're on top of the world

10:11 am You found the rainbow

10:12 am Lucky you

January 10

10:12 am You got out in time

10:12 am Trust your future

10:13 am Chase your dreams

January 17

10:38 am There's something around the corner

January 18

10:25 am A world of possibilities

January 22

10:03 am Life is full of opportunities now

12:03 pm The pain has melted

January 25

8:19 am You're a rock star

Girl Power

From: Sophie
To: Julia
Subject: Girl Power!
Sent: Wednesday, January 28 8:12 pm

Hey!

I just heard the big news! Another girl...?! Wow! Amazing...!
I called your home number just now to say bon voyage for your trip, but Abby couldn't hold back – she blurted out the news with huge excitement.

You would have *loved* having a boy, but there will be such a fun camaraderie in a house full of girls. (But I would start thinking about putting in another bathroom – ASAP ;)

So, as you settle into domestic family bliss (as if taking off to Hawaii is anything like nesting), my own quest continues. I am doing paintball tonight (which Abby has informed me can be very painful. Something they failed to mention on the website). Alone, since I can't get any single friends to join me. I even tried some married friends (yes, for this singles event) without luck.

On the 14th, I am going to The World's Largest Anti-Valentine's party at Schmooze downtown (with 800 of my closest friends). One girlfriend is coming along to that one, which is great.

PLUS, I am hoping to go to a fundraiser on Feb. 15th. On top of all of this, I have started doing the hot yoga on Wednesday and Friday nights. Life is so full right now that my head is spinning!

Cameron is piping up in the background right now, concerned about your baby being born in Hawaii. Be careful ~ you never know, girl.

We've had a great day so far - he scored a hat-trick in hockey this morning, so life couldn't be better :)

Try to get some free time in to enjoy your beautiful surroundings there. With this being baby #3, Hawaii might be a tough place to get back to. (Sad but true...)

Safe travels.

Sophie

From: Julia
To: Sophie
Subject: **Re: Girl Power!**
Date: Thursday, March 1 11:52 am

Sounds amazing, Soph - way to go. You will be able to write about all of these adventures one day ~ a "How to do Life" manual.

It is so glorious here in Hawaii! You should definitely honeymoon here.

(...Or is that bad luck to plan the honeymoon before you've met the groom? ;)

Talk soon,

Julia

February 28

3:42 pm Life is how it should be now

3:43 pm You did it, girl...

3:43 pm You really did it.

Quote of the day, which really should be our lifetime anthem:

A real man will ruin your lipstick... not your mascara.

Unknown

How can something that seems so complex, really be so *incredibly* simple? Imagine the tears I would have saved had I lived by those words two years ago.

From: Sophie
To: Julia
Subject: **shoes**
Sent: Saturday, June 23 7:41 am

Hey, Sunshine ~

I was wondering where you got those shoes that you were wearing the other day…? They were a cross between a runner and a nice casual shoe.

I'm going zip-lining and rappelling tomorrow at the Elora Gorge but I forgot my cross-trainers at school. I thought I could whip out and get something like what you had on - they looked cute and practical all in one.

S

From: Julia
To: Sophie
Subject: **Re: shoes**
Sent: Saturday, June 23 7:58 am

Good Morning ☺

I think I got them at Adventure Feet.

Your idea sounds fabulous - what a great reward after report cards! Who are you going with?

J

From: Sophie
To: Julia
Subject: My adventures
Sent: Saturday, June 23 8:13 am

...Just me. I signed up as a carrot to get me through those mind-numbing reports and as a year-end treat. I was terrified when I went zip-lining over the jungle in Costa Rica but loved the rappelling part, so it may be a bit of a mixed bag...? I'm optimistic that I will come out of it a converted zip-liner :) I figure that anything in Elora will be beautiful, right?

I am going with a singles adventure club that I discovered on-line. I have no intentions of meeting anyone - I've been to a few functions before and it seems to be almost all women. Regardless, I thought it would make for a fabulous day as they really do deliver on fun and excitement.

Next month I am going Treetop Trekking with them. Again, afraid of heights(!) but it looks beautiful. (I really must find another way to enjoy scenery...)

I am hoping to find someone to go tubing with me down the Grand River on July 6th. Interested?? I am sure the whole 9-month pregnancy thing wouldn't get in your way ;) (Can you picture us trying to get you out of the tube?! BTW - Are you sure you're not having twins?)

Wish me luck on Sunday :) (I hope I come back in one piece...)

S

From: Julia
To: Sophie
Subject: **Re: My adventures**
Date: Saturday, June 23 8:22 am

Fantastic! Good for you. I am coaching a woman in one of my courses whose goal is to pull herself away from the TV on Sundays long enough to go for a 20-minute walk. Her ultimate goal is to meet her soulmate, so this is just step one. I wonder what she would think of your agenda! You go, girl!

Julia

---

5 Months Stronger...

From: Sophie
To: Julia
Subject: More chocolate
Sent: Friday, November 9   10:01 pm

Godiva this time. (...From a student who is celebrating Diwali.)

Seriously. What's going on? I still haven't finished the batches I was given at Thanksgiving and Hallowe'en. How much chocolate can one set of hips take? I swear I am not asking the universe for it.

Men, people! It is men that I need...not chocolate!!

S

From: Julia
To: Sophie
Subject: Re: More chocolate
Date: Saturday, November 10   8:13 am

You are too funny - maybe if you stopped visualizing *licking* the men, the universe wouldn't get it mixed up ~

Julia

Christmas Wishes

From: Julia
To: Sophie
Subject: **Do you know this man?**
Date: Sunday, December 23 6:16 am

Hey Soph,

Watcha think? (Read below.) I know you will be mortified at the thought of this, but really...what do we have to lose? How about I don't send it to anyone you know - just to my network of people who have never met you? We've *GOT* to get you a date for New Year's!

Your admirer,
Julia

Hello friends,

Do you know a nice, single guy? No ~ not for me...I'm throwing out my net for a friend. Perhaps an unusual request, but at this time of year, especially, wouldn't it feel good to connect some wonderful people?

There has got to be a guy out there for her. She would make such an excellent girlfriend. She is fun-loving, thoughtful, fit, energetic and loves to ski, play tennis & travel. She is a glass half-full kind of person and is a great conversationalist with an excellent sense of humour. She laughs easily and makes me laugh each time we talk.

She is a teacher by day and spends her evenings being a mom to a beautiful little boy. She loves to make others happy and searches for kind, thoughtful gestures for her friends and her community at large. She's involved in many charitable efforts to help bring picture books to children worldwide.

On top of all that, she is a great cook. She exercises regularly and is very health conscious. Did I mention she is tall and blonde with blue eyes?

Did that description remind you of any single male friends of yours? If it did, write back and let's see if we can make a connection!

Merry Christmas,
Julia

From: Sophie
To: Julia
Subject: Re: Do you know this man???
Sent: Sunday, December 23 9:22 am

Oh my god. Thanks for starting all of those lovely rumours about me, but you can't be serious. You are out of your mind ~ officially this time...! God help me. (Speaking of which, if I should die before you do, promise me you'll read that as my eulogy. And please put all of that on my tombstone. I'm serious. Who wouldn't get into heaven with a recommendation like that?!)

Sophie

Hours...Days...Weeks...

Nothing. No replies whatsoever. Zero. Rien. Nada. Clearly this man does not exist.

Sure, I was still getting hit on by men all this time, but the line, "It was over a long time ago", while still sleeping in the same bed as their wives, just doesn't cut it in my books.

From: Sophie
To: Hockey - Coach Jake
Subject: **Sorry!**
Sent: Wednesday, February 4 11:52 am

Hi Jake,

What a fool I am. I am so sorry that Cameron missed hockey practice on Monday night.

But if I recall, weren't your last words to Cameron on Sunday morning something like "Have a fun week at school!" I heard nothing like "See you tomorrow!" I am in the middle of report cards, so I am a little needy right now. I needed a neon sign telling me the schedule had changed from the usual Wednesday night practice. Was he the only one who missed it? (Maybe I don't want to know...?)

Sophie

From: Hockey - Coach Jake
To: Sophie
Subject: Re: Sorry!
Date: Wednesday, February 4 12:01 pm

Hey Sophie,

I didn't know about it either. I got the club's e-mail late in the afternoon on Sunday, so I had no idea either until then. I hate to say it but yes, it was a pretty good turnout, surprisingly.

Don't work too hard.

Jake

Hey, Soph! Why the pink glow? Julia asked, as she helped Grace wash her hands at the kitchen sink. **Grace, baby – how about you and Cameron take these grapes downstairs and he can help you and Georgia set up our new video game.**

Cameron and I were dropping by Julia's house and what an added bonus that our mutual friend, Lisa, happened to be there as well. This was perfect. I needed an honest opinion and if one friend didn't give it to me, the other definitely would.

Am I seriously glowing? Damn ~ I wonder how long that's been going on for. I am THE worst for blushing. I must have been bright red the whole time we were talking.

Hey, beautiful! How are you? And who is 'we'? demanded Lisa, as she tucked her cell phone into her back pocket.

I made sure the kids were out of earshot before I confessed any of the details. **Cameron's hockey coach, Jake. Urgent request –**

I need you to do the jiggle test on me. Here – give my leg a good whack and tell me how much it jiggles. I demonstrated on Lisa so that she would give me the proper assessment. What do you think? I asked, with a clear urgency in my voice.

Definitely an 8.2. You're good, insisted Lisa, with complete authority.

None of this would have been necessary had it not been for the special hockey extravaganza that Cameron and I had just attended on the outskirts of town. Even the anticipation of it was big. Really big. In fact, I don't know which one of us was more excited when we pulled up to the private estate of Curtis Joseph, one of our favourite NHL alumni. It's hard to believe that a hockey legend has a property so close to us. Our assistant coach won the prestigious two-hour ice time at a silent auction and was generously sharing it with the team. Now, *THAT* is true love ~ Canadian style.

Everyone was pretty quiet as they tied up their skates and got ready for the big event. The usual chitchat was replaced with feisty determination to squeeze in as much ice time as possible. Cameron and his teammates whipped on their skates, grabbed their sticks and then took off in a flash. Make-shift games quickly took shape at both ends of the rink, with bursts of cheering erupting as the boys savoured the moment of playing on the rink owned by hockey royalty.

I had done about three or four laps before I realized that I was literally the only mom on the ice. So, does that make me fun and supportive...or too much of a keener? I couldn't tell. But what I did know for sure was that I was bored out of my mind, skating around the rink on my own. And I hate being bored. It was time to take matters into my own hands, and so I went over to the bench and grabbed an extra stick that was kicking around to try to spice things up a bit.

My son was mortified. I had officially ruined his day by joining in with everyone instead of just keeping to myself on the perimeter. Ahhh...the foreshadowing of the teenage years at its best.

Now that I was in on the action, I was having a great time. All those years of figure skating were finally paying off. Not only did I have a pretty good wrist shot (sheer beginner's luck), but I definitely held my own in the relay races that followed.

I don't even know how or why Jake and I got talking. Somehow, though, we ended up wandering away from the rest of the group during the post-ice pizza party and he fired a barrage of questions my way. His son was gifted and Jake wanted my professional advice on the various options for him. All I know is that our alone-time felt surprisingly good. In a very unexpected way. Sure, he was cute. And smart. And athletic. And nice. But I've done cute, smart, athletic and nice before. And look how that turned out. Jake and I had had several other chats before – even lengthy ones - where I definitely felt a bit weak in the knees, but I convinced myself each time to just enjoy the moment and chalk it up to just that: simply a moment.

Our conversation was interrupted by Cameron running up to me and whispering in my ear that it was time for dessert ~ time to pull out the up-all-night home-made oatmeal chocolate chip cookies and spread them around to the team. The coaching staff all dedicated an enormous amount of time in a cold rink for six months so that our boys could have a bunch of fun and excitement on the ice. Staying up late to bake was the least I could do for them in return. And watching everyone's reaction while devouring my cookies ~ well, it was like they hadn't had home-made since childhood. Watching the men, especially, was practically like watching them crawl back into the womb.

As I relaxed on the bench, waiting for Cameron to gather up the last of his hockey gear, I quietly watched Jake say good-bye to some of the other families. I knew that I shouldn't be falling for him. I'd been telling myself this for a while now, trying to suppress an array of emotions that I was sure would complicate everything. Too messy with him being my son's coach. Plus, life was busy. Too busy. But the reality is that attraction ~ well, it all just seems to be completely out of our control, doesn't it? Right when you try to control it, it takes over with a very stubborn mind of its own.

So, later that day, despite my self-talk to deny my simmering affections, I had to know: what did Jake feel when he gave me a bit of a slap on the leg, impressed by my racing ability at the hockey party? Hence the jiggle test at Julia's house following our afternoon festivities.

This was not a good sign. It was clear that a harmless crush was starting to take a firm hold of my heart.

Lisa's score of 8.2 likely meant a 7.5, realistically. Not bad. Pretty good. But note to self: must do more yoga.

Eye of the Beholder

I tried to keep my mind distracted by the whirlwind of activity that comes with teaching little ones and being a single mom. And yet, another Wednesday night of hockey rolled around, and with it came more butterflies than a woman my age should ever experience.

All of the parents by now had the changeroom routine down to a science: laces done up with brute force, 87 pieces of hockey equipment fastened up tight with Velcro, and then the final click of the helmet snap, protecting our boys to the max. Imagine your body being completely vacuum-sealed in bubble-wrap. But you just can't be too safe when it comes to a bunch of testosterone-pumped warriors on slick ice.

As per usual, I was one of the only moms present. Why the other moms don't like this winter ritual of suiting up the hockey armour leaves me dumbfounded. I love it. Always have.

The one exception this night was a mom lacing up her son's skates directly beside me. Although, given the Fort Knox of winter gear that she was buried under, it is amazing that I even realized who she was. Somewhere beneath an over-sized coat, floppy winter hat and tight scarf was a mom who was almost unrecognizable. It had to be 80 degrees in the changeroom due to the 30 bodies working away, struggling with all the sports gear. So, what was going on?

I gave her a friendly greeting but she faintly whispered back at me, **Shhh. I'm hiding under my hat. I am not wearing any makeup.** Seriously? Please tell me she didn't just say that. I tried to make her feel better, but her insecurity was beyond any compliment I could dole out.

A few minutes later, I was standing in line at the concession stand, salivating over the big bottle of water I could see behind the counter as I stood at the back of the line. Ahead of me was a very petite, stylish woman, speaking with a thick French accent to a noticeably robust man, towering over her. As I looked at her profile, I couldn't help but notice how thick her mascara and eye-liner were. All I kept thinking was, **I wonder what it's like for a man who goes home with one image and wakes up beside a completely different face?**

An hour later, I found out it just happened to be Jake's ex-wife.

I'm sure she looks perfectly fine without makeup. Most of my friends do. Their beauty is simply subtly enhanced by makeup. But here's the deal with me. In high school, I wore everything. And by everything, I mean everything. Eye shadow, mascara, eye liner. Foundation. Blush. And, of course, lipstick. Every day. Every single day of the 7-day week.

Today, nothing. Maybe some subtle lipstick for a special occasion. For instance, hockey practices are now considered to be special occasions, thanks to a somewhat scrumptious coach. But I literally don't own a stitch of makeup anymore besides the lipstick, but for reasons that defy all logic.

You see, when I wear makeup, everything jumps out in a really big way. Mascara, alone, dramatically transforms my entire face. And I am OK with this look. But, then, fast forward to bedtime when it comes time to take it all off and it's a huge shock to my system, almost needing paddles to revive myself. I love myself and my look without makeup...until I wear makeup, then remove it. And that's when I find myself hating every mirror in the house.

But the biggest insecurity of all, when I always used to be completely dolled up, was that I never wanted to be caught without my makeup on when I was out and about. Just like this woman tonight, lacing up skates beside me. So, for no one but myself, I go for the natural look. It still drives my mom a bit crazy, and every now and then I'll hear her nudge, **How about a little bit of blush, Sweetie?**

With me, it is, what it is. What you see is what you get. No shocking surprises in the morning or at the supermarket or at the hockey rink on days that I was too rushed to 'put my face on'.

~

Jake and I somehow got talking during the commotion in the changeroom, again with him wanting the inside scoop on the gifted program for his son. I literally did not notice one single person leave the room, yet we suddenly found ourselves sitting down side-by-side. Alone. Completely and utterly alone. It was the most bizarre experience. How could I have been in such a zone not to notice the evaporation of all the hustle-and-bustle, the noise, the physical bodies? Gone. All of it, all of them...gone, from all around us, bit-by-bit.

It was almost embarrassing when we both realized what had just unknowingly unfolded. We quickly wrapped up our conversation and scurried out opposite ends of the room - Jake to the rink and me to the spectators' lounge...almost as if we had been caught doing something very naughty. And yet it was all so innocent, in every sense of the word.

One Week Later...

Another Wednesday night somehow snuck up out of nowhere, which meant another night of hockey practice. The team also got together on the weekends, but that was usually for games, accompanied by a heightened focus and increased speed to the pre-game routine. But Wednesday nights were always reserved strictly for training practices, and so there was always a much more casual air to them. Hence, more time to socialize with everyone, including coaches. Hence, more time for butterflies.

After we swiftly got our boys ready for the ice, Jake and I both made quick exits, not wanting to set off the rumour mill if we ended up alone together in the changeroom again.

But it did not end there. What I loved about this particular arena was the section of seats up top on the upper level, behind a huge, grand wall of glass. It allowed "the more fragile" to sit and watch the action, but in lovely, soothing warmth. There was definitely no frozen breath to be seen here. (And best of all, no frozen butts.)

This section was a bit busier than usual – likely due to the frosty air outside, driving many to seek warmth rather than sit in the shivering temperature of the rink.

I wanted to sit in the front row, as did many, which meant that I had to scoot down to the far end of the section to find a vacant seat.

As I sat there, nonchalantly typing away on my phone, I casually had one eye glued on Jake. I watched him lead the boys in various warm-up drills to get their hearts pumping and muscles powered up. He leaned onto the top of his stick as he let the boys carry out their shooting drill but what took me by surprise was how his eyes focused on the person at the far end of my seating section. Then, the next person. Then, the next. Then, the next. His eyes moved with such precision down the row of spectators, as if connected to the second hand on his watch.

My heart beat faster and harder as I realized that his eyes were getting closer and closer to mine. What would I do if they got to me? Should I smile? Should I pretend not to notice? Should I pretend not to care?

At the exact moment that his eyes reached mine, the small, inexperienced player on the team smashed into Jake's skates, bringing him crashing down to the ice, barely missing the human missile that blew up our moment in the first place. And so fizzled out the rest of the night, leaving me wondering and feeling lured deeper into his web of confusing and ambiguous signals.

Seize the Moment

Watcha doin'? I asked Julia in my sleepy morning voice. It was our own version of pillow talk that had become a weekend ritual. Me, snuggled under my cozy white duvet. She, on the other end of the line, shivering on a hard wooden chair at Starbucks on a cold winter's morning. Technically it was spring, but where else in the world does it snow in spring? OK, maybe Norway. Norway and Canada are the lucky ones who get snow in the spring.

We have figured out, that, despite Julia making much more money than I do, she actually works fewer hours in a week. But the catch is that she works seven days a week. I am not good at that. I need my two days off to catch my sanity on its way out the door.

Hence, if I ever want to connect with her on the weekends, I have to call her at just the right time, between her business calls and her scheduled webinars. If I want my ounce of girlfriend catch-up, my luck has to be perfect.

As we shared our itineraries for the weekend, something caught my attention in a way that really gave me an invigorating jolt. Her friend, Rebecca, was going over to Julia's house after lunch to do a shortened version of Getting Your Life on a Roll - one of Julia's favourite workshops that she conducts with her clients, all about goal-setting and making positive changes to your life.

Despite being tight BFF's, I actually felt a bit reluctant asking Julia if there was a chance that I could tag along. I have this insecurity about intruding on pre-set plans and the last thing I wanted to do was to barge in on something that was private or personal.

But Julia was all for it. Of course she was! What was I thinking?

'The more the merrier' has always been her mantra.

I got through my morning routine at Mach speed, thanks to some serious kick in my step. There was something special about this workshop ~ I could just feel it.

Being the consummate teacher, I knew that this was an occasion that called for none other than a pack of brand-spanking new markers. For some reason, there is nothing that excites a teacher more. It tickles the G-spot of our brains and ignites our creativity, pushing all of our productivity buttons in the process. If you put a bucket of beautiful markers in front of a group of teachers, it becomes a feeding frenzy. You can get us to do anything - ANYTHING - if it involves working with a fresh batch of every-colour-of-the-rainbow sticks.

I felt really pleased walking up to Julia's house with the Cadillac version of writing tools, until...I saw in Julia's hands the beautiful, elaborate spring wreath that Rebecca had just given her.

I was entirely deflated, all in the blink of an eye. Not that it was a competition. Not at all. I have never worked that way. But it was an instant reminder of my economic reality compared to...well, pretty much everyone else I knew. Perhaps I had to use this goal-setting workshop to strategize how to bump myself into a higher snack bracket, once and for all.

The Workshop

Julia couldn't find her usual roll of white paper, so she poked around her attic and found two rolls of vibrant wrapping paper - the canvas of our hopes and dreams; the custodians of our redirected futures. I loved it. It was like our deepest wishes would be gift-wrapped in pulsating colour and dazzling beauty.

We immediately sat down at the very large and very inviting island in her new kitchen - the fruit of Tim's labour. Being 6'7", he designed everything in their house to be big and spacious. This was the perfect space ~ the perfect arena ~ for our personal brainstorming.

Rebecca and I each unrolled our wrapping paper, both sensing that we were about to embark on a potentially life-altering journey.

One by one, Julia read out her questions, and one by one Rebecca and I set our brains in motion to go in directions never before navigated. It's funny how, once you have kids, everything is about them. Everything is *for* them. Before that...sure, I had dreams. And I even pursued and accomplished a lot of them. Some big ones. Amazing ones. Working in France, Kenya, Jordan...even Australia. But never before had I ever sat down to map them out, let alone identify specific steps I would take to reach each of those dreams. This was definitely foreign territory for me. Domestic for Julia. Foreign for me.

1) Draw a picture of your ideal life in 5 years from now.

I hate that question. I always have. So much so that it made Julia seem bossy. Which of course she wasn't, but I can't believe how paralyzed I felt from the get-go of this workshop. At this rate, I would never make it through to the end. Who actually thinks like that? All I kept thinking was, who can ever know the true answer to this ridiculous question?

With only one other person at this workshop, it would have been a little obvious if I had a) left this blank, given the enormous size of our empty document b) hidden in the bathroom or c) left the house altogether. I had no choice but to plough through and hopefully turn over and reveal some deeply buried potential.

I reluctantly drew a big, beautiful house – much nicer than my actual one, with my loud, drug-dealing neighbours nowhere to be seen in this illustration. My sun was extra-swirly with warm colours overlapping each other and the trees were rich and detailed with multiple shades of green. I had to really fancy it up to make up for the noticeable lack of content: house, sun, trees.

2) My ideal life includes…

I thought I had made that clear in my picture, but apparently Julia was going for the major squeamish effect. It was time I took this seriously. I had burnout in my job as a teacher, despite being born to teach. Love the job; hate the profession, to quote a wise colleague of mine. I picked up a handful of markers and dove right in, giving this workshop the proper attention it deserved. My ideal life includes:

* new job – bring happiness & harmony to others
* a solid, harmonious relationship
* home – nice neighbours, appealing views out my windows
* Cameron – attend the new sports high school
* travel – more frequent visits back to Australia

3) Choose 4 of those and create 4 squares, going into detail for each topic.

Relationship	Career
* Smart, athletic, successful F(socially & professionally) * Emotionally stable * Healthy, fit * Has a strength that can enhance himself & others * Similar values (travel, harmony, happiness)	* Work for a company where my role is to infuse happiness & harmony into the professional & personal lives of its workers * With happiness & harmony comes job stability – justifies the cost to the company (good Return-On-Investment)

Travel	Home
* More frequent trips back to Australia	* Better location * More soothing & appealing neighbours * Quiet...better view out back * Curb appeal, more space

4) Why do I want all of this?

For greater personal success...closer to my definition of happiness:

* harmonious relationships
* good health
* love
* positive influence on others...cultivate potential & happiness in others
* get away from the negative
* live without regrets...live my best life

5) Draw a circle with 8 spokes. On each spoke, write a main aspect of your life. (e.g. family, friends, career, finances, education, health...)

The centre of the circle is a 0 while the outside is a 10. Score on each spoke your satisfaction in that area of your life.

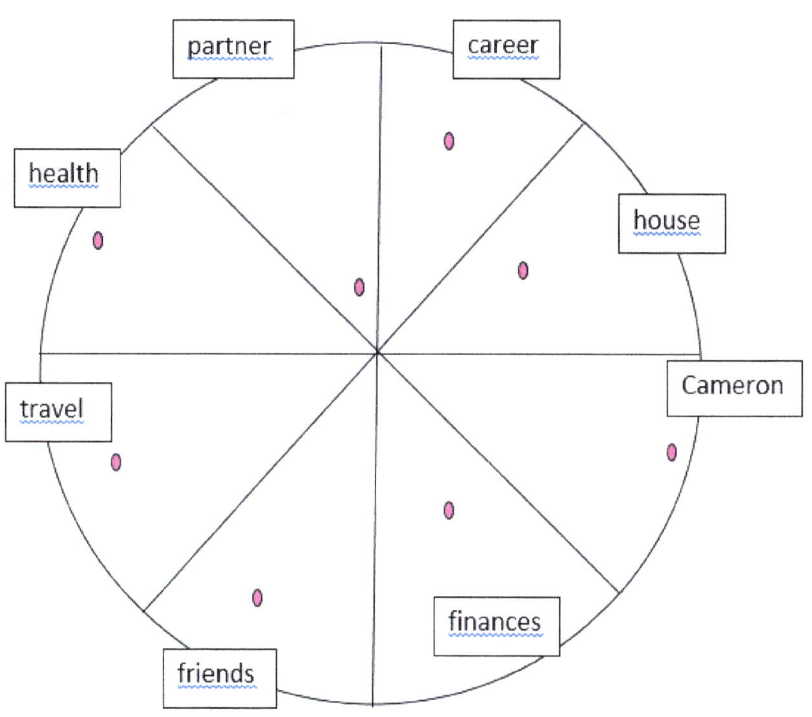

6) Now, create your Wheel of Life by connecting the dots, to establish how smoothly your life is rolling.

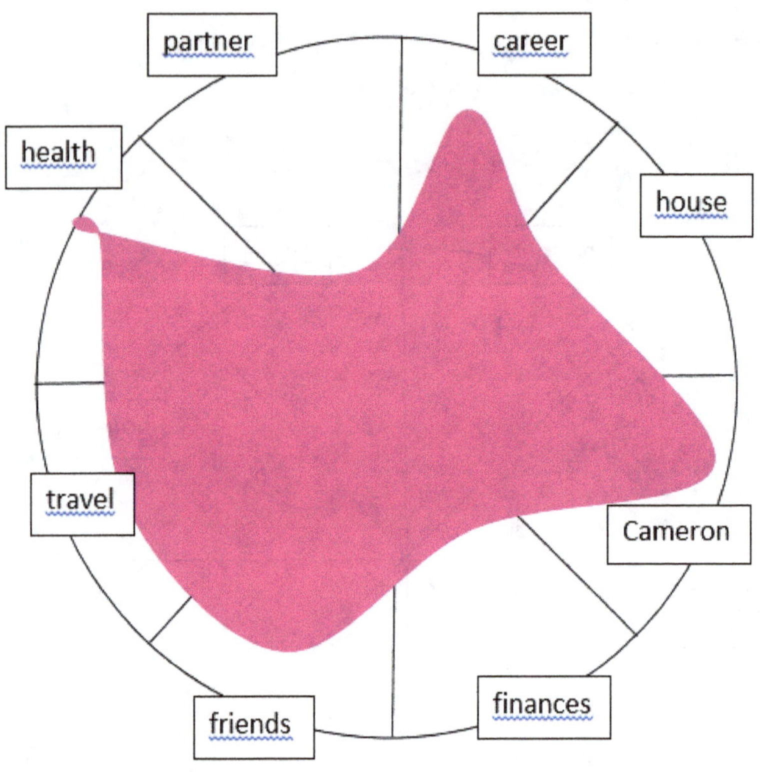

(Hmmm. A squashed marshmallow, trying to roll. No wonder why my life felt so unbalanced. Talk about not having it all...)

7) What do I have to do in order to make my life roll more smoothly?

House – continue culling through cupboards, closets, basement & office...a good selling price will also improve my finances

Partner - focus on self-improvement
- continue networking
- keep going to social functions
- open my heart

8) What strengths & talents do I have that will support my goals?

House – persistence & tenacity

Partner - confidence
- a network that supports & believes in me
- hindsight not to settle

9) What are the challenges that could get in the way of achieving my goals?

House – I am the worst handywoman ever
Partner – turning down men – I hate that feeling!

10) What do I need to do to reach my goals?

House – hire someone handy to help me with the things outside my comfort zone...Steve from Home Depot?

Partner – take advantage of my network of girlfriends (home, work, hockey, soccer) who want to help me...who know I deserve a good relationship

11) What am I going to do today to bring me closer to my goal?

House – call Steve to see if he is available

Partner - set a time-frame – say, 5 dates between now and June 1st ...write an e-mail to my network, explaining this crazy(!) dating idea to everyone

12) What will be your rewards for having the courage to follow through with your goal-setting actions?

House – sell it and move to a whole new house in a safe & calm neighbourhood – I will find my oasis!

Partner – my juicy reward is to have a party at the very end with 5 girlfriends to celebrate my courage and debrief about each of the 5 dates

Run with the Momentum

I left our mini-workshop feeling more enthused than I could possibly have predicted. Julia was amazing. She single-handedly was able to get me to clear away the clutter that was blocking my view of where I needed to be going in my life. And yet, all she pretty much did was read off of a piece of paper. No, not pretty much. That is exactly what she did for about 80% of the workshop. Words that she didn't even write herself. Incredible. Yet, there is no way I could have ever done that on my own. Never. I needed her there, to lead me – no, to drag me, down that path. And having Rebecca present as well – there's no doubt that her silent peer pressure helped to propel me to map out some pretty key ideas. It was a classic case of the force of collective energy and the powers that spill out as a result, slowly but surely, like lava from a simmering volcano.

The ink had hardly dried on my Roll of Life when an e-mail came in from Julia the next morning. At 6:31 am, to be exact. On a Sunday. Who does that? (Oh, right – the woman who makes more money than I do.) How did I ever get involved with this master Yoda of goal-setting in the first place??

From: Julia
To: Sophie; Rebecca
Subject: Dreams really do come true!
Date: Sunday, March 15 6:31 am

...Especially when you turn them into proper behavioural goals. Now that you each have identified your top goal, the key is to do something toward it each day. For example, I dedicate an hour each day to my top goal of publishing my pharmaceutical book.

Sophie - what one small baby step are you going to take today toward your exciting goal of having coffee dates with 5 eligible men by June 1st?

Rebecca - what one small step are you going to take today toward your goal of investigating your exciting business idea such that you have enough confidence to know whether or not to move forward with it by June 1st?

I encourage you each to share updates of your goal with our little support group.

Rome wasn't built in a day but when you are ready and feel excited about it, let's work to create goal # 2. Rebecca, you had a fitness goal sprouting and Sophie, a goal to prep your house to sell it. Let me know when you are ready to activate those goals.

I'm so excited for both of you! You deserve the best that life can offer and you both showed me yesterday that you are ready to go out and get it!

Expect the best! And then make it happen ~

Julia

I sat down to the computer and fired something off because clearly this woman was not going to rest until I gave her at least something to nibble on. So, it was 4 hours after her sunrise. But Julia was proving to be a serious fluke of nature. Computers just weren't meant to be turned on at dawn on a Sunday morning. I think it even says so in the Bible.

From: Sophie
To: Rebecca
Cc: Julia
Subject: Working on my dream :)
Sent: Sunday, March 15	10:32 am
Attachment: 5 Dates

Hi Rebecca,

Thank you again for including me in the time you booked with Julia. What a day! What a future we both have!

I wanted to share with you my 'next step', so I have attached the e-mail I am about to send out to everyone. (This is starting to feel like my personal version of The Bachelorette :) Have a look and let me know what you think. I am open to suggestions – big or small.

Sophie

---

2 Weeks Later...

From: Rebecca
To: Sophie
Subject: **Re: Working on my dream :)**
Date: Saturday, March 30 5:45 am

Hi Sophie,

How goes the bachelorette quest? Thinking of you and hope that you are still as enthused about your quest as the day of our private workshop. Give me an update when you have the chance.

All the best,
Rebecca

From: Sophie
To: Rebecca
Subject: **Still... working on my dream :)**
Sent: Saturday, March 30 7:15 pm

Hi Rebecca,

Great to hear from you. I have not sent out my e-mail yet since I am waiting to see what happens with Cameron's hockey coach. If I am wrong about him being interested, then my radar is way off.

This Wednesday is our last hockey night, so I should know soon, either way.

How about you? Any luck with a treadmill? Hey ~ wait...Happy Birthday?! (Am I right??)

Sophie

From: Rebecca
To: Sophie
Subject: **Re: Still... working on my dream :)**
Date: Saturday, March 30 8:09 pm

Hey there,

Thanks for remembering! B-day is tomorrow – 44...Ughh! :)

Yes! A new treadmill is a special little present to myself...It's coming at the end of the week, although I still need to clean out the garage to make room for it.

I'm happy to say that I have started my research on organic makeup and skincare. I've also finished reading a couple of books on launching my own business. So, I'm well on my way. I did share my plan with my husband and also with two of my friends who are major planners. That was definitely helpful. I also admitted to another 'dance-mom' about my goal for a totally organic cosmetic and makeup line and she was very supportive of the whole idea.

Hope Wednesday evening yields a positive result and that it's something that will keep you happy. Let's stay in touch :)

Rebecca

From: Sophie
To: Rebecca
Subject: **44 ~ hear me roar!**
Sent: Saturday, March 30 9:21 pm

There's your motto to get you out of bed tomorrow. You could easily pass for 38. Hands-down.

Wow. You're doing really well on your goal ~ very inspiring. Keep up that momentum!

Spoil yourself all day tomorrow.

Sophie

From: Rebecca
To: Sophie
Subject: **Re: 44 ~ hear me roar!**
Date: Sunday, March 31 6:22 am

Outstanding! Love that. I was sort of thinking...'44 and out the door'...but I like your sentiment so much better ;)

Keep me posted on the coach front.

Rebecca

Now or Never

As soon as I got home from work, I carefully put together a gift bag for each of the three coaches, with crisp yet fluffy white tissue paper dancing out the top of each one. Always on a budget, plus not wanting my affections for one to be obvious, I had to put my creative juices to work.

Being the hockey nation that we are, it turns out ~ unbeknownst to me ~ we have a limited edition of Oreo cookies embossed with NHL team logos during the playoff season. Of course we do! Hockey rules this country from coast to coast, which now, naturally, includes the cookie aisle. Clever yet understated. It was just what I was looking for.

This final night was a scrimmage between the players with the coaches mixed in. Stress free and all for fun. In the changeroom after the game, it was just Cameron and me, plus a few other kids, left at the very end. The others had slipped out quickly to dive into the pizza party that was building in the front foyer. That suited me just fine as I was too nervous to face Jake, anyway. Even better was the fact that I was able to give Jake's gift to his son ~ one of the kids kicking around the changeroom ~ with the instructions to pass it on to his dad.

I was undeniably nervous entering the party portion of the evening and I couldn't help but wonder how much it showed. How was it, that, as a grown woman, I felt like a teenager all over again? I guess all those songs are right: we really are all just the same inside ~ completely vulnerable deep down to the nucleus of every cell in our bodies.

There was no way I could speak to Jake, being so weak in the knees, so I headed straight over to the assistant coach and the trainer. I handed them their gifts as we made small talk, all the while, subtly noticing the details happening across the room out of the corner of my eye: Jake, off to the side with a stunningly beautiful woman, clinging to his side. They walked over to a nearby bench. Together. This was obviously the girlfriend who he had mentioned way back in January. But he had made it sound back then like it was fizzling out. Clearly, he had found a second wind in their relationship.

And why not. She was a vision. Sure, she was completely buried in makeup, but I have come to realize that some guys (most guys?) don't mind that. After all, I did have that up close and personal view of his ex-wife who was the same – the whole gamut of glamour. On top of it all, this bombshell was impossibly skinny, advertising this fact through jeans so tight that the paint had hardly dried.

I can't compete with that – it just isn't my way. I remember Goldie Hawn, sharing on Oprah's Master Class, a life-lesson from her mother: **Don't be perfect – just be yourself.** And that, I am. Myself. Nothing overly flashy, but, at the same time, no awkward surprises when you wake up beside me in the morning.

Jake placed all of his thank-you gifts on top of the metal bench, but he had something familiar in his hand. It was the card that Cameron had made: a drawing of himself in full hockey gear next to Jake with a whistle in his mouth and puffed out cheeks. He turned to show it to the goddess beside him and they both chuckled over the colourful details. Then, as he peaked into the shiny blue bag and rustled through the fluffy white tissue paper, he burst out laughing at the sight buried within. He loved it.

He walked straight over – thankfully, alone, and gave me a big, huge thank you with an even bigger smile. I melted like soft serve ice cream in the scorching heat. I was instant mush. He spoke to me with such warmth and interest in his voice – maybe I was all wrong about the girlfriend thing...?? Maybe she was just his sister? Cousin? Neighbour? Co-worker?? **Ahhh, Sophie – I love the Oreo cookies – what a great idea! You just made my day.** He held out his hand and said with sincere appreciation, **Thanks for a fun season. Have a great summer.**

I somehow was able to shake his hand back – or maybe my hand simply was just being carried along with the momentum of his handshake. But the rest is a complete and utter blur as I choked on my own breath. He vanished as quickly as he had appeared and I had no other choice but to turn back to my left to listen to the assistant coach pick up on the conversation where he had left off, before Jake had popped himself into our conversation...then out of my life in a flash.

The hustle and bustle from the party suddenly went into an unrecognizable slow motion ~ something I have heard others claim, but never believed. Not only did all the commotion around me get stuck in a vat of molasses, but, so, too, did the voice of the assistant coach beside me. His voice was so sluggish that his words were completely incoherent to my ears, as if we were submerged under water. I literally had to shake my head and say, **I'm sorry – what did you say?** He continued with something about his wife celebrating her 40th birthday this year, so they were heading down south for a big hoopla.

I somehow managed to end the conversation quickly, said my good-byes to him and the trainer, then whisked Cameron out for a smooth and quiet exit.

I was beyond relieved to get outside so quickly as I don't think I have ever needed fresh air quite like I did in that very moment. This was worse than when I was 12. Now, at my age, I knew exactly what I would be missing out on: the late-night phone calls, the texting, the pillow talk, the snuggling. Everything good about a relationship. The hope of it all. All of it, gone in an instant. Like having the rug pulled out from under me at the speed of light.

How could I have been so...so *wrong*? So completely and utterly *wrong*?? I just didn't get it. I prided myself in life on the strength of my instincts. During my teaching degree, I remember doing an in-class activity, having to read a section of the teaching resource The Seven Ways of Knowing, about the seven types of intelligence.

Although we all have the rainbow of intelligences, one stands out as a dominant one in each of us. For Vivienne, it is Linguistic Intelligence. We led cycling tours together in France and I can't tell you the number of times I heard the locals say to her, **So, what part of France are you from? Just south of here?** Granted, she did do an exchange to France during university. But, to be mistaken for a local? That's just crazy impressive.

For me, the activity revealed that mine was Interpersonal Intelligence. I can still see it on the bottom right-hand side of the page: "...often found in people who experienced a serious childhood illness." The meningitis – encephalitis – in a coma – my dad teaching me how to talk again using puppets – all, at the tender age of two. It all added up and made perfect sense.

And one of the strongest features of this type of intelligence is instincts. And wow, have I had them. Mostly ignored, of course:

* The unexpected whisper in my head as I walked towards the chapel, all dressed in white, about to marry the sweetest guy in the world. **(Ignored.)**

* The eerie feeling while I stood at the top of a steep toboggan hill in a winter wonderland, moments before crashing at the bottom and breaking my back in the process. **(Ignored.)**

* The hairs standing up on the back of my neck on a first date, listening to him go on about his insurance fraud. **(Ignored.)**

And yet, here I was convinced that Jake was interested in me, based on so many encounters, but I was completely off-base, all along…all this time. Completely, utterly wrong.

Poor Cameron. I listened to everything that he said on the drive home from hockey and during his bedtime routine, yet I heard not a word of it. I was still shell-shocked. Devastated. Shattered.

Once Cameron was settled for the night, I scanned over Regina Brett's list of 45 Life Lessons and chose the best one for the moment:

When it comes to chocolate, resistance is futile.

She's 90. I figured she must know what she is talking about by now.

I marched over to my shiny red bin overflowing with chocolate and dove right in. Thanks to Christmas and Valentine's Day, there was more than enough stash to get me over this crisis. A few (meaning, several) empty wrappers whipped off at lightning speed was the only evidence of my sugar hit. Wasn't it just last week that I responded with a flat-out **NEVER** to the staffroom survey question, **Are you an emotional eater?** I clearly proved that to be dead wrong in this moment of personal catastrophe. Hell, yeah – a tub of Chocolate Peanut Butter Häagen-Dazs was next on my agenda.

Sudden Clarity

Everything you've ever wanted is on the other side of fear.

George Addair

I was lying in bed on yet another frigid Saturday morning, not wanting to leave the comforts of the warmth of my bed. Julia was on the other end of the line at Starbuck's – she called me this time, with an eager buzz to her voice. Today was the day, according to her. The big e-mail about going out on 5 coffee dates had to be sent to every single person in my contacts. (I really have to start looking for an underachiever as a BFF.)

I'm not ready, I said. **I'm just not ready. The timing isn't right.** The idea was unfathomable. How could I expose myself to every living creature in my world, when I wasn't even over him yet? Wednesday night was a mere two and a half days ago. Sixty hours was simply not enough time to get over being stopped in my tracks like a runaway train hitting a brick wall. How did she not *get* that?

And then...*I* got it.

Jake and I *had* no relationship. There was *nothing* to get over. It was like suddenly waking up from a dream...as if someone had put smelling salts under my nose and snapped their fingers, giving me instant clarity again.

What was I thinking? How could I have been so off base? How could my radar have been so completely...*broken*? But, clearly, he was just not that into me. I had to move on with my life and my quest of finding Mr. Right. I had to listen to Regina Brett's Life Lesson # 36:

Don't audit life. Show up and make the most of it now.

Julia was right – I had to send that e-mail out. Today was the day.

My usual morning routine required an immediate shower, quickly followed by a mandatory breakfast. I don't drink coffee (oh, how I wish I liked it), and so my morning shower *is* my morning cup of coffee. A full wash of the hair is required to drag myself out of my sleepy state into the hard reality that morning ushers in so quickly. It is officially the only thing that wakes me up and gets me going. I swear that there is not an ounce of vanity involved – my hair actually *looks* better the next morning when I crawl out of bed. But put me on a deserted island all by my lonesome and I would still need a full shower with a good, clean scrub of the scalp. (And, yes – I would make sure to be on the only deserted island with hot running water.)

And as for breakfast…I can't tie my shoelaces without it. When I go out for breakfast, I literally have to eat breakfast at home before I go.

So, you can imagine the level of my determination when I threw off my fluffy white duvet and headed straight for the computer in my office, by-passing the shower and bowl of Wheaties in the process. I had already wasted *months* waiting for something with Jake to materialize. And look where it got me. Lying in bed on a cold April morning. Alone. Completely and utterly alone. Julia had lit a fire in my belly and I was not about to extinguish this raging flame.

Now, to be honest, I think part of me thought that this big, momentous e-mail could somehow be sent within about three minutes flat. But sixty minutes later, I was still labouring over the most insignificant details. I can't blame it on the process. Heck, the actual e-mail had already been written two or three weeks ago. No. The gruelling hour was completely self-inflicted. Most of this time was spent painfully deliberating over who would be a lucky recipient, and more importantly, who needed to be intentionally excluded from the list.

Mom and Dad. Definitely not on this A-list. There were certain things a parent wants to know and be a part of. This was not one of them. It definitely was not one of those times in life to be best buddies with Mom and Dad.

Then, there were others who just would not be appropriate recipients, such as parents of my students who had gradually become friends over the years. Definitely too much information for them.

Then there was the reality of it all. Did it sound 'just right'? My God – just how desperate would this appear? Would I instantly lose the respect of my entire support network?

As I finally...*FINALLY*...pushed that oh-so-difficult 'send' button *down*, with perfect synchronicity came the sensation of my cookies about to be tossed *UP* and *OUT*. Hard and fast. This task of entirely putting myself out there in the most vulnerable possible way – well, it felt like it was, without a doubt, game over for me. I was now officially exposed, from top to bottom, inside and out. And it was the most awful feeling imaginable. It was so emotionally difficult that my head was spinning and I wasn't certain I would be able to avoid passing out and making sudden contact with the floor in the process.

From: Sophie Edwards
To: Philippa - kiwi girl; Charlotte; Vivienne; Allison; Mr. Yip; Myriam; Mary Liz; Margaret; Lucy; Louise; Lindsay; Maria; Beth; Marcelle; Emma; Jane; Janice & Scott; Kate – life coach; Fiona; Diana; Debra; Julia; Danielle; Carolyn & Terry; Carol; Ian; Karen; Rebecca; Lisa; Jennifer; Bettina; Emanda; Sharon; Elissa; Hockey - Coach Jake
Subject: 5 Dates
Date: Saturday, April 4 12:35 pm

Dear friends,

Spring is in the air and what better time to seize the renewed energy that comes along with it.

I just attended a fantastic workshop that focused on two things: analyzing the areas of your life that you want to change or improve, and setting goals to achieve those changes. It made me realize that I am long overdue ~ it's time to start dating again.

I set a goal to go on 5 coffee dates between now and June 1st... I'm just not sure how I'm going to find the men to go on those dates!

So, that's where you come in. Dig deep. Do you have any friends or colleagues who are single and who might be compatible with me? Maybe go through your address book and see if it triggers any names.

Is this crazy? Definitely! But you never know where it could lead ~ at the very least, a fun exercise in goal-setting.

Looking forward to hearing from you ~

Sophie

Somehow, with the help of a designated angel above looking out for me, I managed to stay upright and carry on with my morning routine. Although...why would it matter anymore what I looked like, or felt like, for that matter? And smelling fresh-as-a-daisy, suddenly, no doubt, had become necessary strictly for my own tolerance. Because, surely, not only would I be date-less, but the rest of my social life would come to a sudden halt. The smell of desperation must have become insanely intense to all of my recipients, just with the push of that 'send' button. I was sure of it. Regina Brett suggests,

When in doubt, just take the next small step.

I had defied all logic and her sound advice by rebelliously taking pretty much the biggest leap of faith known to mankind. Exaggerating? I suppose. But it sure felt huge. And reckless.

But then tip # 23 is a whole different ball game:

No one is in charge of your happiness but you.

If I made this my personal motto, then I could say that I was being a model student. Mr. Right was not going to fall out of the sky onto my lap. I had no choice but to put it all out there and see what the universe delivered back to me.

For me, this was the ultimate fear of the unknown. I was completely relying on Regina's tip # 40 as if it were written in stone:

The best is yet to come...

The Fruits of Our Labour

Whoever said that anticipation was half the fun was either lying or had never waited for anything important in their entire lifetime. The next 3 hours and 5 minutes were the longest of my life. And that is coming from a woman who went through 25 hours of labour with a nine-pound baby in a foreign country. So, trust me. I know long. I guess the issue for me was the fact that sounding desperate to the entire world tends not to be on the Top 10 List for what most guys are looking for these days.

From: Philippa - kiwi girl
To: Sophie
Subject: Re: 5 Dates
Date: Saturday, April 4 3:40 pm

Hey sexy gorgeous woman!

Damn that I missed your call yesterday. I was out at a wedding. I really didn't want to go at all as I'm sick of watching other people get married...!

What a great and brave idea doing this 5 Dates thing. I can't think of any single men here in New Zealand or else I'd take them myself!

I hope your friends on that side of the world come up with some nice options for you. GOOD LUCK & let me know how it all goes.

I'm off to Noumea a week tomorrow, so that will be a nice break. Maybe I'll meet a nice single man there?!!

Talk soon, my friend.

Love *Philippa* xx

Seriously? She LOVED the idea??! I suddenly felt a thousand pounds lighter. And happier. And verified. I love you, Philippa!

From: Charlotte
To: Sophie
Subject: Re: 5 Dates
Date: Saturday, April 4 4:43 pm

Sophie,

I read "coffee dates" and said to myself... Oh, that sounds nice! I read further and realized I'm not invited.

So, anyway, how does this sound:

"Hi Jake... Just checking in as your hockey league convenor...I still need your team evaluations handed in. It would be great if you could let me have them early next week. I know your equipment got handed in...I think you owe Sophie a coffee. (I think she likes the atmosphere at Second Cup :) Cheers, Charlotte"

I'll keep thinking. Bob from next door is still available, but he is complicated. Not horrible, just complicated. Which might be intriguing...maybe?

Charlotte

OK – so that is two. Two people who do not think I am certifiably crazy. So, if all else fails and everybody else thinks I am utterly nuts, I will have Charlotte and Philippa to hang out with. So, one of them would have to be on Skype every time... at 3 am due to the time change to New Zealand. No big deal, right?

Maybe this wasn't such a bad idea after all...?

From: Rebecca

To: Sophie

Subject: Re: 5 Dates

Date: Saturday, April 4   5:23 pm

Hey Soph,

OK - I've got a great guy. He's interested in going out on a coffee date with you. His name is Marcus and he is fun, attractive...he loves life, he's in good shape, AND, he's a really nice guy. I told him that we were friends, and that the reason for this e-mail request is because of our recent goal-setting workshop.

He was on that corporate weekend retreat with my husband and me, so he totally understands life-planning and goal-setting.

Even if nothing comes from this...he is a really fun, interesting, nice guy.

Good luck and enjoy!

This was fantastic, but what the hell?? Was this THE very same Rebecca who did the goal-setting workshop…*with me*? There were two of us participating. In total. Side-by-side. Three weeks ago. And yet, she was appearing in my in-box as if this was the first she had heard of this dating project. *And* that I was single? How was this news to her???

My only guess is that she was focused on her own goals at the workshop, as I am sure I was with mine. I remember the advice Julia gave me when I separated from my husband. You see, I was never the kind of person to get divorced – we were always good to each other, even behind closed doors. So, I was petrified of what people would think of me for getting divorced.

In one fell swoop, Julia summed up the reality of life. She said that, when people hear my tragic news, they will be heartbroken and distraught – maybe even hold my hands in despair for a few brief moments...before they turn around and say, **Tell me ~ does my butt look fat in these jeans?**

The e-mail I sent out must have put Rebecca into *my* zone, helping her to isolate her busy thoughts, just long enough to come up with a smashing idea for my own life-altering goal. Regardless of the how and the why...who cares - I had a bachelor! **Bachelor # 1** officially exists!

By this point, Julia and her three daughters were over for dinner of what my mom used to call catch-what-you-can ~ a hodgepodge of food thrown together with the hope that a full meal would result. Cameron had been over at his dad's for the weekend, but popped back home to join us for what was guaranteed to be a fun night.

There was no way he'd miss out on any occasion with them, as Julia and her crew have become like family to us. Our kids are like siblings. No ~ cousins. They don't fight, so definitely not siblings.

For Julia to see first-hand the exciting results of her coaching was so fitting, but also pure luck. This dinner tonight was not planned and it's safe to say they rarely ever are with us. Our very best times together have always been spontaneous. Her husband, Tim, was still busy finishing up the final touches of their reno of pretty much doubling the size of their house, and I had become Julia's go-to girl to cure her boredom. With me being her only single friend, I was pretty much guaranteed to be available at a moment's notice. Call it a symbiotic relationship.

Furthermore, how could I have ever predicted the speed at which people would respond? Who knew that I would have my first of five dates within hours of going public with this man-plan of mine? There is no way in a million years that I could have foreseen such an amazing response. I would have done this *years* ago had I realized just how easy it really was. What was I so afraid of? I don't even remember anymore, to be honest.

From: Lucy
To: Sophie
Subject: Re: 5 Dates
Date: Saturday, April 4 6:06 pm

Hey! I think this is a great idea! My little town is full of singles. Some lucky guy is waiting, I just know it. Talk to Lauren...She will have some ideas for sure.

I have lots to say but no time in which to say it. My husband is at the soccer game with a friend and I have the girls here with lots of questions. Both are hungry & tired after a full afternoon of errands, so I should get going.

I will be in touch soon but I fully applaud this idea! Very creative. I want to hear more about the workshop - I could use some inspiration!

Lucy

From: Sophie
To: Lucy
Subject: Re: 5 Dates
Date: Saturday, April 4 6:10 pm

Thanks for all your amazing words! But tell me - as long as your girls' questions aren't about my big e-mail??!

Sophie

From: Lucy
To: Sophie
Subject: Re: 5 Dates
Date: Saturday, April 4 6:27 pm

Absolutely not!!! I assume it was intended for a private audience. I can't wait for our swim sessions with cocktails – how many months 'til summer?? ...Snow on Monday :(

From: Sophie
To: Lucy
Subject: **Re: 5 Dates**
Date: Saturday, April 4 6:33 pm

Yes, not for little ears! Thanks for keeping it discreet.

O.K. - the single men in your town - are they not all players and cheaters? Someone asked Lauren for my number last week but she (thankfully) won't give it to him due to his frequent shenanigans.

Such crazy weather. Hurricane winds here all day.

FYI - I already have a date! Can you believe it?!

From: Lucy
To: Sophie
Subject: **Re: 5 Dates**
Date: Saturday, April 4 6:47 pm

Yes - I can totally believe it! You're a hottie! I'm still thinking...
Lucy

I don't know what first made me put my hand on Cameron's forehead. Maybe it was a look in his eyes. Or a quieter demeanour. Or maybe just plain mother's intuition. Sure enough, he was warm.

Too warm. Then my questions began which then confirmed my suspicions. Sore throat. Aching head. Yucky all over.

It was time to pack this party in. With three of her own along for the fun, I am sure the last thing Julia wanted was to catch something from Cameron and have it rip through her household. And so, with the efficiency of an army sergeant, Julia whipped potluck dishes into tote bags, cleaned sticky little hands and smooshed hats and jackets onto each of her disappointed kids. All, while I held Cameron as he melted further into my arms as the fever took a deeper and deeper hold. He would be fine; we just had to ride out the symptoms and let this bug run its course. I sat us down on the steps, Cameron still draped across my body, and replied to Rebecca while Julia did her final bit of gathering:

From: Sophie
To: Rebecca
Subject: Re: 5 Dates
Sent: Saturday, April 4 6:57 pm

Wow!! Thank you! You were my very first result! Julia is here with the kids so your timing was perfect. You completely made my day!

Must deal with Cameron and his fever right now, but more soon. Lots to tell!

Sophie

From: Rebecca
To: Sophie
Subject: Re: 5 Dates
Date: Saturday, April 4 6:59 pm

Oh Geez. Hope Cameron is OK. Fevers are the worst.

I love that you are doing this. You are so brave and I admire you so much! You go, girl.

FYI - I do have a really good track record with introducing people. No pressure, though. Wink, wink ;)

Rebecca

I stood up to see them off, but just as Julia was on the verge of ushering her little troops out the door, the fairy dust sound on my phone went off again. Another e-mail. Any other night and I would have let it slide. There was chaos and commotion that was about to evaporate in a matter of seconds, once they were gone. So, why the whispering in my head for me to pick up my phone?

Women's intuition this time? Or just plain addiction to that glorious, magical sound that had been bringing such unexpected words of encouragement for hours now…

Regardless, I somehow managed to bend down, with over-sized child in arms, reaching for the third step where my phone was casually resting. I gently touched the e-mail icon that would change everything.

My eyes have never been wider; my knees, never weaker. My head was spinning, not knowing a time I felt so filled with such complete and utter disbelief.

Julia was barely three feet away, face to face with me, bursting with curiosity. Without hesitation, I twisted my phone around and held it up to her face for her to see with her own eyes the impossible that was just delivered into my in-box:

From: Hockey - Coach Jake
To: Sophie
Subject: Re: 5 Dates
Date: Saturday, April 4   7:01 pm

Can I be the first?

Judging by the look on her face, it was a toss-up as to which one of us was shocked the most. But simply put, I could not have been *more* shocked. Thrilled, yes, but dazed and confused as well, all in one twisted tornado of emotions.

You sent it to...Jake?? *COACH* Jake???? What were you *thinking*????? laughed Julia.

I know! How crazy is that?! OK – look. Hear me out. I figured he made it *crystal* clear that he was not interested in me, right? Not only did he never ask me out when he had ALL the opportunity in the world for months. *MONTHS!!* But he shook my hand! He shook my hand at the last night of hockey and said, Have a great summer! Could he have been any clearer? That is saying good-bye to me for six friggin' months!

Luckily, Cameron was asleep on my shoulder by this point and Julia's kids were drowning out our voices as they rubbed their shiny winter jackets against the front door, competing who could be the loudest. As a result, we did not have to speak in code as we normally would when speaking about matters of the heart – *my heart* – in front of the kids.

OK ~ I get that part, she rushed, swooping her hand in a circular motion, trying to get the answer out of me as quickly as possible.

So, I am done with him, right? And, I figured...he's - a - guy! I might as well use him as a resource. He works in corporate downtown – he's got to know guys in suits. He plays hockey AND soccer – he's simply got to know some single men, right? Somewhere, there have got to be single guys! I figured he would know some! That is how desperate I am. I sent the most vulnerable e-mail possible to a man who I have been crazy about for half of the hockey season. I figured this was no time for insecurities or inhibitions. Or sanity, apparently. I heard your voice in my head telling me to do it!

Oh my God, she laughed, throwing back her head, You're a rock star! My work here is done! I have taught you well, girlfriend. I'm so proud of you, I could cry!

Oh my God! He actually wrote; Can I be the first? I KNEW it! I knew my radar was right. I should never ignore my gut. But what the heck? Is he coming or going? Bloody hell! He shook my hand and said, Have a great summer! Who does that? Who says good-bye like that to a girl you actually like? My God. I was right - none of us actually mature beyond the age of twelve when it comes to all this stuff.

OK ~ listen, she whispered, as she noticed Cameron shifting in my arms. We should go and you have to get your little guy up to bed. Let me know what happens!

I poured Cameron into bed and I sat down on the floor, leaning against his bed, to take it all in and reply to Rebecca.

From: Sophie
To: Rebecca
Subject: Re: 5 Dates
Date: Saturday, April 4 7:31 pm

Hey ~ me again,

Thanks for all those words of encouragement, sweets. They mean more than you can imagine. Believe it or not, mustering up the strength to go ahead with it all this morning was excruciating...and then I was suddenly weak and nauseated and exhausted all over as soon as I hit that send button.

But fast forward a few hours and the rest has been spectacular! E-mails have been pouring in, all full of wild encouragement. I've even heard from Cameron's hockey coach, which came as a total shock. I would highly recommend this to anyone single. Now, looking back, I don't know why it took so much courage. It had to be done, right? We all know that I'm long overdue to start dating again and so it was time to take action.

Your friend, Marcus, sounds great, so I will follow up for sure. It's good - no, amazing - to suddenly have options!

I'll keep you posted :)
S

I was completely stumped as to what to write back to Jake. This was way too much responsibility for someone in my state to handle.

From: Sophie
To: Hockey - Coach Jake
Subject: Re: 5 Dates
Sent: Saturday, April 4 10:02 pm

You're technically the second. But, given that you are a 'friend of the family', I could bump you up on the list if you like…?

From: Hockey - Coach Jake
To: Sophie
Subject: Re: 5 Dates
Sent: Saturday, April 4 10:24 pm

I guess being the coach has its perks!

But seriously, after I sent the message, I thought it was the wrong way to respond and was about to apologize, but I'm glad you replied.

I was going to call you tomorrow, if that's OK…?

How is your evening going?

Jake

From: Sophie
To: Hockey - Coach Jake
Subject: Re: 5 Dates
Sent: Saturday, April 4 10:39 pm

It was a bit of a crazy night. Friends were here for a spontaneous dinner which was very fun. Cameron was with his dad this weekend, but joined us for dinner since these friends are like family to us. Then he came down with a fever, so the night ended early and he is staying with me. Nick's a great dad but I am more of the doctor between the two of us, so I wanted to be close to him in the night.

Had any cookies lately?
Sophie

From: Hockey - Coach Jake
To: Sophie
Subject: Re: 5 Dates
Sent: Saturday, April 4 10:48 pm

Too bad - I heard there's a lot going around. Hope he feels better, Doc ;)

Max is here with me, too. I have to admit - it felt kind of empty without hockey today. It will take some getting used to, now that the season is over.

I've had a cookie (or two or three). Thanks to both of you - that was definitely a very fun and creative gift to all the coaches :)

(Here I am writing to a teacher and I'm sure my spelling is horrible.)

From: Sophie
To: Hockey - Coach Jake
Subject: Re: 5 Dates
Sent: Saturday, April 4   11:07 pm

I know what you mean about hockey. While you were slaving away on the bench, the rest of us got to socialize non-stop. I can't believe how strong our hockey network has become over the years.

I should get to bed. But, BTW - your spelling is perfect. How about you don't worry about your spelling and I won't worry about the quality of my hockey the next time the parents are on the ice. Deal?

Sophie

From: Hockey - Coach Jake
To: Sophie
Subject: Re: 5 Dates
Sent: Saturday, April 4   11:11 pm

Deal. Have a good night and I'll speak to you soon.

From: Sophie
To: Philippa – Kiwi girl
Subject: OMG
Sent: Saturday, April 4 11:15 pm

Philippa!!!

I already have 2 dates - can you believe it?? One is with the hockey coach whose last words to me on Wednesday night were, Have a great summer! So, I thought it was pretty clear that we had zero future together.

And then he replied to that insane e-mail of mine, wanting to be the first in line.

You have to do this, Philippa! Just all of the fun responses from everyone have made it such an ego booster! Do it!

Love & hugs,
Me…!

From: Philippa – Kiwi girl
To: Sophie
Subject: Re: OMG
Date: Saturday, April 4 11:27 pm

Ha!!! I saw Jake's e-mail address there and that's exactly what I

I thought! I knew he would reply – I absolutely knew it!!! You just had to put it out there. I am so excited for you!!! Jake is the man - I just know it.

If I did this little dating project here in New Zealand, there would be no takers and certainly no hockey coach waiting in the wings. Forget it!

Love you.
Philippa xxx

As It All Sinks In...

Sunday morning. I should have been sleeping in but my heart and mind were pumping full of adrenaline. I turned on my phone first thing, before my eyes even opened, as per usual. I find the stimulus that I get from contact with the outside world is much more effective at waking me up than any alarm clock I've ever tried.

And sure enough, there was an e-mail from Julia. She had forgotten her phone here last night and she was outside, waiting for me to wake up.

Are you serious? How long have you been sitting in my driveway? I whispered, as she tiptoed in my front door.

Not long at all – the timing was good. I was just sitting there for a few minutes, sipping my chai tea latté, enjoying some rare peace and quiet. Here – I brought you one – you'll love it – it's my new favourite. Soooooo....how *are* you???

Dreamy...absolutely dreamy. This 5 Dates idea is amazing! Why didn't we do this ages ago? What was I so afraid of?? Seriously? What was it?

Ummm...humiliation...rejection...feeling exposed, looking way beyond stratospheric vulnerable.

Oh, yeah. That. Well, it couldn't be further from the truth. This is just crazy fun. Thank you for making me do this! Jake and I wrote back and forth for ages last night. But I made sure that I was the one who cut it off, so that I didn't seem, you know, too desperate.

Yeah, babe – way too late for that. You just sent an e-mail out to everyone you know asking for dates. I think he knows you're desperate. Hey, listen - I should get going. My cell phone – did you find it?

Oh – yeah. It's right over here.

As I handed her the phone, I could tell something else was on her mind.

I think you need to forward your 5 Dates e-mail to Rebecca's bachelor today. Thank him for playing along and propose some possible dates for coffee.

But...

DO IT! Look, just because you are having coffee with Jake – hey, I just think you should still follow your goal to completion and not put all your eggs in one basket. I know it would be easier to just meet with Jake, but I've listened to some reservations about him over this past winter and you won't have this type of momentum in a few months, if or when he doesn't work out. So just stick to the goal. That's my two cents worth.

I hugged her good-bye and admitted, I hate it when you're right.

As I closed the door behind her, the e-mails kept coming in...

From: Kate – life coach
To: Sophie
Subject: Re: 5 Dates
Sent: Sunday, April 5   9:18 am

Congratulations, Sophie, on setting this fantastic goal! I will dig into my contact list and - better yet - my husband's contact list.

Question for you...who do you consider to be compatible with you? I have never met anyone you've dated, so I need some info to go on.

Good luck with it all! You had to know I'd be all over this ;)
Kate

From: Sophie
To: Kate – life coach
Subject: Re: 5 Dates
Date: Sunday, April 5 9:37 am

Hi Kate - nice to hear from you!

Thanks for thinking of me. Within a few hours of sending out the e-mail, I already had 2 dates lined up. This has been the most incredible experience - more fun than you could possibly imagine. I'd highly recommend it to any of your clients.

Even if nothing comes of it, I will have a long list of e-mails to refer back to, reminding me that I took the bull by the horns and didn't just let life pass me by. Julia was here for an impromptu dinner last night, so she was able to see all of the e-mails come flying in. (Did you figure it out that she was the one who led that workshop? Informally, with Rebecca as well, but she is following through with it like I am a high-paying client.)

My type? Hmmm...Let's see. Smart, athletic, good sense of humour, successful in their career, someone who has a good track-record with relationships...(Isn't this what we all want?)

We never did organize our winter get-together at Julia's 'palace'. And, look at that – it's already spring! My reward, once I reach my goal, is to have a party with a bunch of girlfriends and debrief everyone on the 5 dates. You should come! It is guaranteed to be loads of fun.

Hope all is well with you. Your little guy must be so adorable - I remember those days where you hang off of every word they say and want to record every waking moment. Unless, of course, he is already in the terrible 2's...? Cameron hit them right on schedule, as if someone whispered in his ear "ready-set-go" the night before his birthday...

Sophie

From: Kate – life coach
To: Sophie
Subject: **Re: 5 Dates**
Date: Sunday, April 5 10:21 am

Hi Sophie,

I would love to join your debrief party! No doubt that you're going to have huge success with this project. Yes - I assumed Julia had something to do with the idea of a concrete goal around dating. She is amazing at getting us to take action.

My son just turned one last week which gives me 12 months of bliss before those tantrums set in. I'm trying to savour every minute of it :)

Hope to see you soon.

Kate

From: Sophie
To: Charlotte
Subject: **You won't believe it**
Sent: Sunday, April 5   10:29 am

Charlotte – please tell me the truth - did you e-mail Jake???

Because, he replied to that e-mail I sent out to everybody – he actually wants to be one of my bachelors. Can you believe it? (Please don't repeat this to anyone - especially at the rink.)

As for Bob next door to you, you're right – I've heard from another friend that he is complicated. Sadly, I have already had a lifetime worth of complicated (...all from one guy).

But thanks for the idea. I promise not to turn down any other suggestions ~

S

From: Charlotte
To: Sophie
Subject: **Re: You won't believe it**
Date: Sunday, April 5   11:01 am

Don't worry! The only person I've discussed your situation with is my older brother. He's part of the cowboy network, and he had only one guy in mind.

Think...**the last living human**.

So, the other two guys I thought of were:

Mr. Eligible #1: High school chemistry teacher, divorced, three boys about the same age as my kids, lives here in town, owns a sailboat (think...summer :)...brings nice wine to parties, enjoys talking to women.

Mr. Eligible #2: ESL teacher who travels frequently to Japan, has his own business and does some freelance work...not currently married but that's all I know about his marital history.

I'm sure that you're curious about all the cowboys that I deal with. I'm sorry, but there is no way a man who buys his clothes from a store called "Cowtown" is going to be compatible with you, especially when you see what is splattered on that clothing by the end of the day!

From: Margaret
To: Sophie
Subject: Re: 5 Dates
Sent: Sunday, April 5   11:16 am

Hey Soph,

As I'm reading your e-mail...I'm thinking 'Great...let's get together for coffee!'...Then I realized...opposite sex - I get it! Ha!

I'll dig through my address book. Great way to network!

Margaret

From: Sophie

To: Margaret

Subject: **Re: 5 Dates**

Date: Sunday, April 5 11:24 am

That is so funny - Charlotte did the same thing. Thanks for thinking of me. Hey - good news! I already have 2 dates. But Julia is the one coaching me through this and she will not rest until I have met my quota.

Yes - we are due for coffee! Thank goodness for Charlotte's pie parties or we would never see each other. My reward, once I have reached my goal, is to get together with a bunch of girlfriends and debrief Bachelors 1 through 5.

You should come!

Sophie

From: Margaret

To: Sophie Edwards

Subject: **Re: 5 Dates**

Date: Sunday, April 5 11:49 am

I'm in!

M :)

~ And So It Begins

The time had come to take this project to the next level. And here I thought the hard part was over. Surely there has got to be a personal assistant out there that I could hire for tasks like this…?

From: Sophie
To: Marcus
Subject: hello :)
Sent: Sunday, April 5 11:55 am

Hi Marcus,

Rebecca gave me your name (and a glowing report ;) and suggested that I contact you. I'm not sure how much she told you about what I'm doing, so I've attached the original e-mail.

Let me know if you are still interested ~
Sophie

From: Marcus
To: Sophie
Subject: Re: hello :)
Date: Sunday, April 5 12:56 pm

I know what you're doing...Hopeful that our coffee date will be epic...lol...Where do you live/work?

From: Sophie
To: Marcus
Subject: Re hello :)
Sent: Sunday, April 5 1:04 pm

I guess this is my version of internet dating – but much safer this way...? I live in Applecross and teach at the north end of the city. What about you?

Sophie

From: Marcus
To: Sophie
Subject: Re: hello :)
Date: Sunday, April 5 1:15 pm

I live in Belmont and work as a lawyer downtown...What do you teach?

You've got my number from Rebecca, right? Call me.

From: Charlotte
To: Sophie
Subject: chem. teacher
Sent: Sunday, April 5 1:21 pm

Sophie,

This is what I sent to the chemistry teacher...

Hi Keith,

I'm not sure if you have a "significant other" these days or not. My friend, Sophie, is divorced and just getting back into dating. I thought of you when she sent the e-mail below. I think you'd like her a lot. She's a Grade 3 teacher, has one son, and lives in Applecross. At worst, you'll have a nice coffee date with a lovely woman who you can chat with at the rink.

If you're interested, you can give her a call or send her an e-mail. Her contact info is attached.
Charlotte

...I'll get more info about the ESL teacher when I see his sister today. Yes, his mom and sister both live here in Applecross. No travelling across the countryside every Christmas!

Charlotte

(P.S. Hmmm. "Every Christmas." Am I getting ahead of myself?)

From: Charlotte
To: Sophie
Subject: no luck
Date: Sunday, April 5 1:33 pm

Sorry...that e-mail address to the chemistry teacher bounced back. I have done some searching and it appears he has moved to the other side of the country for work :(

BTW – I like your approach to this whole life issue of finding a mate. I don't think it makes sense to set a goal of "entering a committed relationship by such and such a date" - a bit like my sister-in-law's crazy stories of girls she went to high school with. They had banquet halls booked for wedding receptions even though they'd never met Mr. Right. Okay, being desperate is a bit warping, but REALLY!

I do have fantastic news, though. My brother's widow is getting married. I am thrilled beyond belief. Our whole family is thrilled beyond belief. Her new partner is a wonderful man. Rock solid and realistic. We all adore him and want the best for them. He is, coincidentally, her kids' school principal and she was his mentor principal, believe it or not. This is such a scandal that both of them have left the Catholic School Board and become principals for the public board. The Pope will have to deal!

Charlotte

From: Sophie
To: Charlotte
Subject: **Thank you!**
Sent: Sunday, April 5 1:44 pm

Wow - you're good. Thank you for doing this and for your amazing words about me (...all just gossip on the street started by me ;)

You can't imagine how quickly all this is happening. My head is spinning out of control and I almost don't know how to handle all of this attention. The e-mails are flying in, mainly congratulating me on my crazy level of courage.

No need to stop painting your kitchen for this - I do have until June 1st :)

Sophie

P.S. Great news about your sister-in-law! That family deserves to be happy. I guess love really can strike at any age...any stage. Very, very inspiring, especially for a woman like me who is looking for love when I am hardly a spring chicken.

From: Charlotte
To: Sophie
Subject: **Re: Thank you!**
Date: Sunday, April 5 7:30 pm

As I was typing, I thought about how much fun this must be for you... but a bit scary, too, yes? You're amazing to be able to say "out loud" that this is what you want out of life. Many of us say our most superficial wishes the loudest, and our deepest (and most important) wishes never get announced.

Good luck with all the coffee dates. As I said to Keith, the worst is that you'll have a lovely visit and a new face to say hi to at hockey or around town.

Which reminds me ~ if anyone suggests a guy called Randy, you must say no. He's one of the hockey coaches, and he is a bit more complicated than Bob next door. He's a bit more complicated than your ex-boyfriend, if you can believe it.

You have good friends, so I'm sure it won't come up.

You are going to have 50 dates by June 1st! Have fun with it!
Charlotte

Since Jake's son was with him every weekend, including Sunday night dinner, I knew he wouldn't be calling until later in the evening. Had I not known this, the day's wait would have been excruciating. I was so busy, though, receiving and sending e-mails which definitely helped with the passage of time throughout the day.

But once dinner, bath and bedtime were over and done with for Cameron, I didn't seem to have the same strength and stamina to wait for Jake's impending call.

Finally, the lengthy silence in the house was broken by the sound I had been waiting an entire 24 hours for. As soon as call display showed that it was him, an instant injection of courtship adrenaline shot directly into my veins like a runaway horse.

I thought I would be all jittery when we spoke, but my nerves quickly relaxed into a surprising calm, once I heard his voice. It was an easy conversation, thanks to all of the time we had spent talking in the changeroom at hockey. But, it's as if I suddenly had some new-found confidence, thanks to the barrage of compliments coming in with all those e-mails from my collection of cupids.

We laughed a lot, starting by dissecting the insanity of my big dating project. He thought it was incredibly brave of me going public with the whole idea. I suggested he try this **5 Dates** thing, but he insisted that, despite having the courage to try out for the NHL years ago, he was not up to the challenge of announcing to the world that he was looking for love.

He was really busy with work, having to go to New York and Montreal for conferences, so we agreed to connect later in the week to fine-tune a window in our schedules. I hung up feeling very...content. Very at ease. Very comfortable with the vulnerable state I had projected myself into, so abruptly…so blindly.

I somehow ended up sitting on the kitchen floor during our conversation without realizing it and couldn't help but notice after I'd hung up the phone that Coconut's dish was still full of his dinner. He had turned his nose up at his kibble, yet again. It's our own fault, really. We took the advice of our butcher early on and put him on the raw food diet of fresh uncooked meat and veggies. Naturally, he took to it like a duck to water. But then, when we took him to the vet for his routine vaccinations, she demanded up and down that we take him off of it immediately. It would just be a matter of time before we killed our darling little puppy via salmonella poisoning or a sliver of bone perforating his gut, according to her. I've no idea if she was right, but I do know that she put an irreversible fear of God into me. I could not take the risk. Boring, dry kibble it would have to be.

Sadly, he has been a food snob ever since. And rightly so. It is hard for anyone to taste caviar then have to revert back to Spam.

Without really thinking it through, I picked up a piece of kibble out of his dish and skimmed it across the floor like we were playing a game of crokinole.

Shock of horrors! Not only did he go after it, but he actually ate it. So, I did it again...and again...and again...and again, with each piece being devoured as if it were the best thing he'd ever tasted.

I was then reminded of the little trick he plays with other little morsels that I toss to him every now and then: a blueberry, a carrot stick, a piece of my morning cereal. Instead of eating the tiny snack right away, Coconut will pick it up with his teeth and throw his head back, flinging the treat in the air in the process. He somehow never gets bored of this self-inflicted game of cat and mouse.

This was all it took to trigger my light bulb moment of the century: **It really is all about the chase, *isn't it*?** This was big. Really big. How could I have been so naive all along? Jake finally got involved when there was some competition involved. The ultimate chase. The ultimate aphrodisiac.

I wanted to call Julia straight after my call with Jake, but she follows the old adage 'early to bed, early to rise' religiously. Instead, I sent her an empty e-mail with only the subject heading **I have news**.

I thought I would be wide awake, bursting with excitement from the weekend, but I was so exhausted from my 5 Dates circus act that I was asleep before my head hit the pillow.

Monday

When I turned on my cell phone in the morning, it was literally ringing with the first bit of juice it tasted.

Is it about Jake?? whispered Julia, trying not to waken a house full of bodies still catching some more shut-eye.

I have upgraded my coffee date with Jake to a drink. With alcohol. I could hear her quietly squealing from my update. **Long chat last night. We may be destined to be just buddies, but time will tell.**

Wait. Wwwhat??? OK - not what I was expecting. Why just buddies? OK – I may sound disappointed, but this could be good. Turning over stones is important. Better to find out what is best than to go in the wrong direction with the wrong guy.

But – hey – I took the leap of faith and made contact with Marcus. Just by e-mail, but it is a start.

Now her squealing was no longer a whisper. **Oh, this is good. Really good.**

Oh – and I have started inviting people to the end-of-goal party. Kate, Margaret, Charlotte. Is this counting my chickens or just good plain optimism?

No – I love it! Looking forward to it! Presumptuous that I will be invited?

Apparently it's at your house.

Well, then - I guess I'll be there!

I was about to hop in the shower but instead grabbed my phone again to follow up with a quick e-mail to Julia:

From: Sophie
To: Julia
Subject: ...thank you :) :)
Sent: Monday, April 6   7:11 am

Seriously ~ I can't thank you enough for all of this. What a shift, eh? I guess my struggles of the past...what? Four years? Over. Done. Thank God, for your sake! Hard to believe you hung in there.

I can't imagine how fun this has been for you, knowing that you are responsible for ALL of this. I am going to have a great day because of you.

Enjoy all the snow!! (Is it really April or did we skip spring, summer and fall?)
S

From: Julia
To: Sophie
Subject: Re: ...thank you :) :)
Date: Monday, April 6   8:00 am

I'm so glad you feel like this is a new beginning – perfect timing, being spring and all. This is the new you - going out and getting what you want in life - and having fun doing it!

I'm loving every minute of this, being your wingman. I'm here for you, girl! Thank YOU for sharing your journey with me.

Make it a terrific week! (Keep sizzling, you ;)

Julia

It was one thing to get all those e-mails on the weekend, but now that I was back at work, it was torture not to be able to constantly check my in-box and respond. After two full days of a steady flow of e-mails coming in, I was officially addicted to the fairy-dust sound that went off with each and every delivery. I was literally starting to feel withdrawal symptoms, longing for that sweet, delicious sound and the amazing affirmations that accompany it. I was increasingly developing a newfound respect and sympathy for all the addicts out there. My skin was crawling for lunchtime to come so I could finally check my phone for enchanting treasures.

From: Lindsay
To: Sophie
Subject: **Re: 5 Dates**
Date: Monday, April 6 11:53 am

Well, it's about bloody time! This is absolutely a great idea!!

Put yourself out to the universe, girlfriend. If you don't ask, you won't get.

We'll put our thinking caps on...

Lindsay

I had to wait until after the 3:30 bell for my unexpected treat:

From: Hockey - Coach Jake
To: Sophie
Subject: hope you're having a nice snowy day...
Date: Monday, April 6 2:56 pm

Sophie,

It was great chatting with you last night. I hope your day is going well...? I worked from home today as I was feeling a little too lazy to drive downtown in all this snow.

So, I found out a few things about you - mainly that you're a cheap date. (See what men remember?!) LOL. I want to know a little more before our cheap night out ;) You've intrigued me a little and I am curious in nature...so don't hold back.

I know you're in school now but would love to hear some more when you have time.

I patiently (but painfully) waited until Cameron was sound asleep before I tackled this one. I had an amazing past – leading luxury cycling tours in France, doing archaeology with Harvard in Kenya and Jordan, teaching and having my sweet baby boy while living in Australia - but it was hard to go into it all without sounding pompous. I took the short-but-sweet route and went light on the details as I typed away with my thumbs, all the while being embraced by the white fluffy bubbles of a steaming hot bath.

Tuesday

From: Danielle
To: Sophie
Subject: **Re: 5 Dates**
Date: Tuesday, April 7 8:21 am

Lunch. Saturday. Say yes! I want to get the whole scoop on this dating project of yours and I figure we should do it over some good food.

BTW – are you *crazy*? Who the *hell* has put you up to this? Let me rephrase that: who the hell is *making* you do this?? I think I'd rather remove porcupine quills from a rabid skunk than go out on 5 blind dates. I'm starting to think that you have more courage than brains, Soph. (But, having said that...I want every single, microscopic detail.)

Sorry to disappoint, but I have no names in my address book to suggest – or at least none that I would ever let near you.

Danielle

From: Sophie
To: Danielle
Subject: **Re: 5 Dates**
Sent: Tuesday, April 7 1:00 pm

Lunch sounds perfect! Let's work out the details closer to

Saturday. I can't wait to hear how you've been spending your year off from teaching – just be gentle when rubbing in the envious details.

S

From: Charlotte
To: Sophie
Subject: **Fwd: 5 Dates**
Date: Tuesday, April 7   3:47 pm

Hi Sophie,

Here's the correspondence (below) with William. His nephew is in Grade 5 with our boys and plays hockey with them as well. He's an interesting guy - an ESL teacher and, as he says, he's moving to Japan where he has lived before.

In the spirit of short-term goal-setting, I thought that you'd still like to drink coffee with him...? He's nice and easy to talk to.

Charlotte (see below)

From: Charlotte
To: William
*Subject: **Fwd: 5 Dates***
Date: Monday, April 6   9:14: am

Hi William,

I received this e-mail (see attachment) from a friend of mine this this weekend and I thought of you. If you're interested, let me

know. I think you should go for it!
Charlotte

From: William
To: Charlotte
*Subject: **Re: 5 Dates***
Sent: Monday, April 6   9:44 pm

Hi Charlotte,

Thanks for thinking of me. I must be upfront that I am making plans to move overseas. I am waiting for a working visa to go back to Japan and might spend the summer in Europe before ultimately heading back to the Far East. It is not 100 % confirmed yet, but I am hoping that's how things pan out.

I think I would disclose that to her first, as I don't want to waste her time. I would imagine she is looking for someone more settled here...? But I will leave it up to you what to do.

Cheers,
William

From: Charlotte
To: William
*Subject: **Re: 5 Dates***
Sent: Tuesday, April 7   7:39 am

No, really! I think she's just interested in coffee. She'd enjoy meeting you. She has also traveled extensively and so you'd have a lot in common.

Charlotte

From: Sophie
To: Charlotte
Subject: Re: 5 Dates
Sent: Tuesday, April 7   10:18 pm

Hi Charlotte,

I still might pursue this - it would give me practice without any of the pressure, right? I will wait a few days as I am already corresponding with Jake and another guy. I think if I add any others into the mix right now it would be too emotionally confusing. (I guess this is a sign that I'm not player material...?)

At least everyone involved knows what is going on. I think it's actually making the men more attentive because they know there is competition. But it's almost starting to feel like "be careful what you wish for"...

Thanks for everything. You've been amazing!

S

From: Charlotte
To: Sophie
Subject: Re: 5 Dates
Date: Tuesday, April 7   10:47 pm

I think you should take the perspective that it's all fun. Jake's been going slowly all along, and maybe he's playing it safe as well...?

Look around ~ see what's out there. You might decide that a few "just friends" relationships is all you need while you get used to the idea of dating again...

Charlotte

Wednesday

From: Sophie
To: Rebecca
Subject: Marcus
Sent: Wednesday, April 8 6:28 am

Hi Rebecca,

A quick update for you on Bachelor # 1... Marcus and I have e-mailed each other and have tried to connect with each other by phone. (Great voice, BTW.) I googled him and you're right – he is definitely attractive.

Hopefully we'll talk in the near future and set something up. Stay tuned!

Sophie

From: Rebecca
To: Sophie
Subject: Re: Marcus
Date: Wednesday, April 8 6:51 am

Oh!!! I have goosebumps. I'm so proud of you for following through with this.

That's too funny that you googled him. He did actually ask me for

for a picture of you. But in the true spirit of what you are doing, he said he didn't need it.

This is so cool. Have fun and enjoy. You rock!

Rebecca

It was 5:30 pm on Wednesday, and while sitting at my desk at work, the name that kept showing up under "missed calls" was finally appearing in my call display. This was good news. There was no hope of anything beyond coffee with William due to his plans to move back to Japan. But based on e-mails and Rebecca's endorsement, **Bachelor # 1** was sliding smoothly into that Potentially Mr. Right spot.

Hello? I asked, with pure optimism.

Little Miss Soph-ie! Hey - it's Marcus.

Hi there! We finally connect by phone. That telephone tag was getting out of control.

You can say that again. So, tell me about this whole dating thing - Holy sh*t. Fk! That bastard just cut me off! Jesus Christ. These city drivers are freakin' nuts. Sorry about that – where were we?**

Ummm....I can call you back if this is a bad time?

No – not a problem. I'm good. I'm just weaving in and out of traffic during rush hour here. So – this 5 Dates thing – I like it! Whose idea was it again? Sh*t – hold on – it's my mom calling.

(F**k! Jesus Christ...bastard...holy sh*t. OMG. What was that?! Apparently I don't get out much? I must be way too hung up on first impressions – clearly I am too reserved. Looks like the new trend is just to throw it all out there. Except, I don't have that much personality in the best or worst of times to throw out there ~ even if I were ever to be rip-roaring drunk..!)

Yeah - hi. Sorry about that. Pickin' my mom up for dinner and she was just checking – fk – hold on again – last time, I promise. It's my sister.**

(Holding...holding...still holding...)

OK – so, coffee! Yes – let's do coffee. Come down to Belmont. I know this great little café tucked away and then we can take my – Bloody hell! One more time – I'll be right back – I promise...

(This guy needs elevator music on his cell phone.)

OK. Coffee – Saturday – 2:30, and we can take my dogs for a walk in the ravine. Sound good? You in?

I'm in! I said, with as much enthusiasm as I could muster up, giving a partial, unimpressive fist pump in the air to try to convince myself as much as him.

Great. I'll text you the details. Ciao, Bella!

Whoaaaaa! How many espressos does it take to keep up with that?! I was exhausted and that was only a two-minute conversation...with most of it being put on hold. OK – that's it. I decided right then and there that Saturday would just be a 20-minute date. Hi...how are you...nice to meet you...Wham, bam ~ thank you, Ma'am…'Don't let the door hit you on the way out' kind of date.

From: Sophie

To: Danielle

Subject: Oh no!

Sent: Wednesday, April 8 6:35 pm

Hey Danielle,

What a crazy day today – it was indoor recess, thanks to the torrential downpour, and my students were bouncing off the walls all day long. I thought I was going to go out of my mind! Missing work? One lunch with me, baby, and I will be sending you into early retirement. Guaranteed.

OK – major update on Marcus – Bachelor # 1. Contact has been made. Help!! He is too much for me!! Such a high flyer - swings in high circles and swears like a trucker. I can already tell that I am not smooth enough...I am just not...I don't know – grown up enough? City slicker enough?

Damn it. I was optimistic about this one. I will still do the right thing and go out with him. But I am terrified!! I just have no clue as to how I will hold my own with such a fast-talker...

S

From: Danielle
To: Sophie
Subject: **Re: Oh no!**
Date: Wednesday, April 8 7:31 pm

Ooooooh – be careful of those smooth operators, Sophie. Are you sure you want to go through with this?

Danielle

Jake!!! Where are you? Why couldn't you just be dates one through five???

I was so torn. I was starting to wonder just how utterly foolish this whole idea was after all. Yet at the same time, the support just kept pouring in, conflicting my emotions even more.

From: Vivienne
To: Sophie
Subject: Re: 5 Dates
Date: Wednesday, April 8 7:42 pm

Hi Sophie,

5 Dates? What a *great* idea! I love it! Why didn't I think of that?? I just know that there is a wonderful guy out there looking for you. It happened to me when I was your age and so I have a very good feeling about this.

We leave tomorrow for our big trip to France. (Ahhh, yes ~ Paris in the springtime...) Have a wonderful Easter and give that beautiful son of yours a great big hug from us.

Love
Vivienne xo

P.S. Ben wants to know if 'coffee dates' is code for 'casual sex'. Because, if so, he says he knows a couple of guys here in town ;)

From: Sophie
To: Danielle
Subject: Lunch!
Sent: Wednesday, April 8 10:28 pm

Me again,

I forgot to mention - Marcus is a go for 2:30 pm. He suggested coffee and a ravine walk with his dogs. (I actually thought that part was kinda sweet...?) This might not be so bad after all...? Maybe he'll have given up swearing by then...?

So, that makes it easy for us to meet for lunch before my eventful Date # 1. I like what you said a while back about Eat It Up Café, near your place. (Love the name, BTW.) Interested?

S

From: Danielle
To: Sophie
Subject: **Re: Lunch!**
Sent: Wednesday, April 8 11:15 pm

Sounds perfect. I can meet you at the restaurant at noon.

Let me say, Sophie – as crazy as I originally thought this whole dating project was, I'm starting to warm up to the idea. I'm sure it was really hard to go through with it all, so, way to go. I came across this quote today and thought of you:

"Love is everything it's cracked up to be...It really is worth fighting for, being brave for, risking everything for. And the trouble is, if you don't risk anything, you risk even more." Erica Jong

Looks like you know what you're doing after all :)

See you soon.

Danielle

Bachelor # 1

From: Sophie
To: William
Subject: Hello :)
Date: Friday, April 10 11:50 am

Hi William,

Charlotte told me that she filled you in on my goal to start dating again…? I know that you are likely moving overseas, but she suggested (insisted!) that we still get together for coffee.

I think she is right. It would be good for both of us, especially since there is no pressure involved.

If you are interested, I think that my best option for me this weekend would be today sometime, if that works for you…?

Sophie

From: William
To: Sophie
Subject: re: Hello :)
Date: Friday, April 10 12:25 pm

Hi Sophie,

How about around 1pm…? But given that it's Good Friday,

I guess a lot of places are closed. There's a Starbucks on Stirling Hwy just north of the liquor store. The atmosphere is warm and cozy, which we definitely need on a day like this. What do you say?

Also, please feel free to come casual as most of my better clothes are in Tokyo.

Cheers,
William

William...Date #1 of my ambitious dating assignment. Marcus, at first, held this initial spot on my dance card, but things suddenly got put into a blender and Date #1 with William was coming at me with the speed of a runaway train.

I must say, though - getting ready for our date was likely the least stressful pre-game experience of my life. There was zero pressure, thanks to international circumstances: how many guys have the excuse to wear jeans on a first date because all of their best clothes are on the other side of the world? I was elated when I read his 'dress casual' instructions due to this very original geographical excuse. Well played, William. Well played. Plus, the fact that he was moving back to Japan in a matter of weeks took all the stress out of it, thereby guaranteeing me at least a few moments free of nervous babbling. That's got to be worth showing up for.

It felt like William came out of nowhere...sort of. Yes, there had been some rumblings about him from Charlotte over the past few days, but between 11:50 am and 1 pm - all of one hour and ten minutes on a frosty Good Friday, William and I met electronically, corresponded five times and dated. My God. What woman has not spent seventy minutes going through her closet, trying to figure out what to wear on a date?! It's a miracle I had anything on but my underwear when we met for coffee. It can take me ten minutes, alone, just to decide which fancy panties to select for a special occasion like this. We really should have a cheat-sheet for dates, breaking it down into specific categories. Blind Date. Dinner Date. Third Date. Break-Up Date. Granted, it was just coffee today. But, still - the decision is ridiculously drawn out even when we know FOR SURE that they will never see our finest lace. According to Regina Brett, the most important sex organ is the brain. And I'm guessing that "which style of delicate panties to wear, even if no one else will ever see them" must fit under that rationale. I know that if I look sexy - even just to myself - I feel sexy, ergo I radiate sexy.

~

I was late. I wish I could say on purpose, but, sadly, no. It's better that way, though, right? Be the last to arrive? As the woman, if I were to be on-time for a date – or, even worse, early...wouldn't it smell of slight desperation? If I were to arrive first, wander around to every man in sight, only to come up empty, imagine how thrown off my game I would feel before the date even started. I say it is best to leave the man wondering, hoping...salivating. It occurred to me that this really should be in the rules book. Note to self: Be late for all **5 dates**.

I pulled into the relatively empty parking lot at Starbucks ~ my new office ~ and quickly found a spot. Not directly out front, of course. That wouldn't allow me the liberty for a final once-over in the rear-view mirror. Hair? Teeth? Lipstick? Check. (Who knew that's what those mirrors were *really* designed for.)

I opened the door of the coffee house with a remarkable amount of confidence and composure. This wasn't so bad after all. Why was I so nervous...no, terrified(!) to hit that send button on my original e-mail?? Talk about anticipation being the worst part. But, now that I was (almost) in the thick of this self-reinvention plan, I felt fine. Completely fine. Seriously - what was all the fuss about?! **Bachelor # 1**? Bring it.

As I spotted him from across the room, all I kept thinking was, **Long distance relationships get such a bad rap. I mean, come on - how bad could the flight to Japan *really* be?** It's extraordinary how a split-second encounter can trigger a whirlwind of emotions and instantly carry us off to some far-off fantasy land. As our eyes connected in that magical moment, I smiled and pointed to him – not in a John Wayne kind of way, but in a lady-like, question mark kind of way.

Within a blink of an eye, I could tell by his expression that he had no idea who I was or what I was talking about. None. Whatsoever. I got a **who-the-hell-are-you...you're-freaking-me-out** kind of look from this man who I had decided in a split second was - without a doubt – my future husband. My world eventually stopped spinning...just long enough to set my eyes on the real William, sitting at the table to my hard left, completely primed and raring to go. I would say in a cheerful eager-beaver kind of way, with his tight, wavy blond hair and his casual dress shirt hugged by a beige argyle vest. He had a bit of a sexy-nerdy-professor vibe going on. Happy. And nice. Even without opening his mouth, I could tell that he was nice.

He stood up to greet me and nonchalantly took the initiative of buying me a coffee. Ahhh…a true gentleman. Clearly his mother had raised him well. Not that I would have minded paying the $2.60 to buy my own coffee. But gentlemen – if you are listening: when out on a coffee date, buy the coffee. It is a bit like opening the door for someone – it is not expected, but it goes a long way and sets just the right tone to the date.

As we danced through the small talk, not only was I proud to have taken this plunge, I was amazed. This was *soooooo* easy…like a hot knife cutting through butter. I instantly became my own inspiration.

We quickly got hooked on the topic of travel and working abroad, which is where we pretty much lingered for the duration of our time together. Soon into the date, I could tell that I would not be racking up frequent flyer points to Japan, but...such is life. This was definitely worth it. My coffee date virginity was gone and it was painless and delightful. Who knew?! It felt like, if all **5 dates** were this comfortable and this successful, I'd be swimming in caffeine for the next 6 weeks, doing backflips off the diving board.

From: Sophie
To: William
Subject: **coffee**
Date: Friday, April 10 3:24 pm

Hi William,

A huge thank you for being such a good sport about my Bachelorette project. And thank you for being my first! You have set the bar high for the remaining bachelors by being so natural and easy to be with. It's amazing how much we have in common.

Good luck with your adventures that lie ahead. I really hope it all goes well for you :)

Best,

Sophie

From: William
To: Sophie
Subject: Re: coffee
Date: Friday, April 10 3:56 pm

Hi Sophie,

Thanks for your thoughtful message. I think your idea is visionary. One advantage of being a man is that it is acceptable for men to take an initiative, but a woman gets chastised for it. I think it's healthy and admirable that you have decided to simply disregard such conventions and blaze your own trail.

It was nice to meet you and you are right that we have many commonalities. I have friends in the area but all downtown. So, it is nice to have met someone local who is not family. Please feel free to contact me again on whatever basis you feel comfortable with.

BTW - I can be a good sounding board regarding men. I tend to never date women from work and so my female colleagues ask me all the time for advice about certain men. Shows like Sex in the City offer some sage advice but often omit a man's perspective which can skew overall gender impressions and mislead.

Hope this helps...

William

An afternoon playdate with Julia and her kids turned into another one of our 'spontaneous-is-the-best-way-to-plan' dinners. The timing was perfect as it meant that she was able to get hot-off-the-press details of my first coffee date.

For me, the evening was like a free therapy session to bring me down from all the emotions involved in launching this interactive phase of my assignment. We talked and ate and laughed until it hurt. All of the lonely nights as a single mom suddenly became worth it in exchange for the constant flow of endorphins that erupted the day I hit send ~ the day I truly took matters of the heart into my own hands.

From: Julia
To: Sophie
Subject: **thank you!**
Date: Friday, April 10   8:29 pm

Hey Sophie,

Thanks so much for sharing your company and your house with us tonight. I think my girls are ready to move in. (I can have them packed and ready to go by 10 am, if that works for you? ;)

You are so kind to tolerate my "tornado" that I bring wherever I go. So sorry about the mess we created and the ink on the carpet! I will look for some miracle cleaning product. (Seriously – will you *ever* have us back??)

It is so good to have friends that turn into family. We really have a nice lesbian family thing going on here! (Without the sex, of course ;)

Have fun on the next installment of Sophie Edwards' Man-Plan tomorrow. I was going to say "good luck" but that doesn't make sense. No need for luck - you are just out to have fun. Just promise me that you'll be open-minded about this next guy...

I'm so glad to be a part of this awesome, empowering goal-setting project of yours. You really are a superstar for going through with all of this!

Talk soon.
Julia

From: Sophie
To: Julia
Subject: **Re: thank you!**
Date: Friday, April 10 8:50 pm

Such appreciative words! You're right - we really are lucky. But a friend of mine says "you make your luck" and hasn't that been the case with us? This friendship has evolved slowly over time and we've both put a lot of attention into it. Thanks for seeing me through so many challenges that life has thrown my way.

And now, look at our reward ~ enjoying the fruits of our labour by laughing...constantly laughing. Which we deserve. We have earned this, girlfriend.

Scout's honour that I will give Marcus a clean slate – I have already forgotten (recovered??) from our cell phone encounter (drive-by?). (Kidding!)

Oh – and don't fuss about the carpet. My mom insists that hairspray will get it out. (Do they even sell that stuff anymore??)

Sophie

Saturday morning ~ but more importantly, prep time for Date # 2. This day came far too quickly for my liking, due to an intense fear of the unknown. I'd never met anyone like Marcus before and I just didn't see how I'd be able to keep up with him.

I was incredibly nervous getting ready: dressing, undressing, re-dressing, adjusting, accessorizing. Despite the fact that I was completely shell-shocked by his "let it all hang out" approach on the phone, I somehow was feeling completely compelled to impress him from head to toe. Consequently, my bedroom floor looked like a bomb blew up my closet. What was wrong with me? Why was it so important to me to look so good for him when I had a massive hunch that we were not destined to head down the aisle together? I was starting to think that I needed a full-fledged psychiatrist on speed dial.

At least my day would start with a guaranteed fun catch-up session with my colleague. Danielle said that she was taking a year off from teaching to finish up her master's degree, but I couldn't help but wonder if having to deal day-in, day-out with our power-hungry boss helped make the timing rather urgent. We were all so jealous when she got a year-long hall pass, exempt from the unpredictable temper tantrums and crying fits that the rest of us still had to face at work from our boss. I couldn't wait to live vicariously through her details of blissful days of grown-up academia.

~

Walking up to the restaurant was spectacular. This section of

Toronto was notorious for its stunning display of fresh cut flowers for sale, each bouquet vying to stand out from the rest. I have to say ~ it is definitely one of my favourite spots in the city. It never gets old.

The restaurant was a vibrant mustard yellow inside, breathing figurative sunshine on each of the patrons who were still having to ooze patience for proper spring weather to arrive. I rarely go out for brunch and so I was thrilled to see my go-to favourite of Eggs Benedict on the menu. It didn't disappoint; nor did the company. Danielle and I were colleagues first, but our steadfast friendship was the icing on the cake.

We lingered on the sidewalk chatting after lunch, knowing that it would be a while before we would meet again. We parted with a warm hug, then I savoured the extra few minutes I had to spare, pouring over the beautiful array of flowers. They must have covered the sidewalk for a good 50 metres or so. Oh, to live across the street would be an absolute dream. Imagine waking up to that view every morning. After much deliberation, a dozen pink roses, each petal kissed with a slightly darker trim, had my name written all over them. Sold.

Next, came the challenge of getting my car washed. Why-oh-why didn't I think about that while I was still out in the suburbs, where there was a carwash every three blocks? I searched and searched...and searched, and finally found one that was squished tightly between two unassuming buildings. It definitely felt shady, as if it was barely a legal business. Manoeuvring my car into the washing bay was unbelievably tricky and I narrowly avoided scratching up the front bumper. Oh, the things we do for love. But desperate times called for desperate measures, especially when it comes to first impressions.

Thanks to my new and improved G.P.S., it was easy to find the quiet street on the other side of town...and there it was ~ a cute little café, just as he promised. The butterflies started to intensify, which, of course, is par for the course for a first date. Surely the first impression that Marcus gave me over the phone was completely off base. Let's put it down to a bunch of miserable circumstances, after another. After another. I am sure he was really embarrassed.

I got to the café to discover that I was the only patron anywhere in sight. I paced a bit, trying not to look like I was pacing. Oh, the chaos in my head. Should I sit down? Should I keep pacing? Should I zip out and then re-enter? Luckily, I quickly realized just how pathetic that last option was on every conceivable level.

As more and more time passed, it was getting a bit confusing – after all, he did live just down the street. With every male who approached, my excitement amplified...which then fizzled as they walked past the café and out of sight for good. Ahhh! A man with two dogs – I had forgotten about the dogs. But this couldn't be Marcus. This man was dressed like he was about to rip out drywall in a dusty old basement. The voice in my head became the words on my lips: **Please tell me this can't be him. Definitely not Marcus.**

Yup. It was Marcus. I guess "dress to impress" must be so passé. You see? This is why I need to do this 5 Dates thing – I need to learn the *new* rules of dating. Apparently, there is a fresh, updated standard for casual – a new chic, we'll call it. (For example, a 5 o'clock shadow has become the new sexy, even on the red carpet.) Hey - that's OK! There has got to be a plus side to all of this swearing and dressing-down of his. Every strength has its weakness, right? So, every weakness surely must have its own strength, right...? Right???

We shook hands and I have been traumatized ever since. You know how they say that we only use about 12% of our brains? Well, Marcus makes you realize that the rest of us are only using about

12% of our personalities. To summarize him in a word...would be impossible. His list of descriptors fills a page. But in short, he is a trooper. A comic – the Eddie Murphy kind that swears like a trucker. Extremely smart. Wild...wild...and I do mean wild. His lines come out at lightning speed, making it impossible to keep up. He is on to his third line by the time you come up with a comeback to his first line. He is refreshing and exhausting all in one breath. He is delicious and poisonous, all rolled into one - like a deep-fried Mars Bar with the whole mouth-watering thing going on, but you know it is sinfully lethal.

He started the date by socializing – at length - with the owner of the café. He finished the date by socializing – at length - with a couple of buddies who had strolled in – his favourite regulars at the café. In between, he texted. Every 90 seconds. Sending, receiving, setting up Easter dinner with his ex-girlfriend. Like I said...refreshing! I finally politely asked him to turn off his phone and I must say, he was a perfect gentleman. He switched it to vibrate. The messaging continued. Like I wasn't even there. All I kept thinking was, **I washed my car for this??!**

Oh ~ don't get me wrong. He was interested. Very, very interested. Not only did he start talking about our next date – an upcoming bachelor and bachelorette auction – but, he had it all planned out. I was to wear a black strapless dress. I was to get rid of my bangs, which he pushed up and off my face to confirm that he was correct. Why-oh-why was I hiding behind them was his biggest concern.

Then, there was the sex. Offered right then and there. At least it was suggested in a somewhat decorous way, but first he had to figure out where to put his dogs while we were having sex at his place. As he thought out loud to himself, I think his final decision was that he would tie them to the leg of the coffee table. (Wow! The confidence! I like a man who is self-assured...but, seriously?) It was like a one-way conversation, as if I wasn't even in the room. Flattering, hilarious and frighteningly outrageous, all in one.

I kept asking him if I was being punked, frequently looking around at the ceiling corners of the café. When I wasn't stretching my neck looking for a hidden camera, I was trying to find the audio button on my new phone. **Surely there must be a record button on this thing...?! Because there is no way I'll be able to remember all of this.** I literally said it out loud. A lot. It was that obvious to...well, the entire human race, that this was absolute mania. Fun as all hell. But true mania. It was almost like getting a litre of espresso directly through IV. I suddenly came to the realization that I had been living life in the slow lane. Practically in park.

I mean, really. How many women have their hair rearranged on a blind date? And how many get their biceps tested for strength on a blind date? Or - my favourite - are told to stand up so their date can see if they do, in fact, have that tear-drop shape to their quads? Wahoo! I passed the test. Who knew? (I really must add that to my CV.)

I wasn't sure what to do when it came time to pay the bill. Sometimes, that unfolds naturally and organically and most of the awkwardness gets avoided. I was under the impression that it made a guy feel all manly inside when they paid for the date. And given that my share came to all of $2.35, I figured I would give Marcus the opportunity to let his testosterone kick in.

Well, according to his screeching body language, spoken with piercing authority, I could not have been more wrong. Who told me this dating tip? How could I have been so mistaken?? I could practically hear the "Hmmmfff" that was blasting in his head. Ooooh. Things just got a little chilly in here.

Thankfully, the uncomfortable awkwardness was short-lived. Remember that statistic that a guy thinks about sex every sixty seconds? Well, that was pretty much the distance from the cashier to the curb, so he had recovered from my apparent insult by the time we said good-bye. Now, imagine the silliest-ever caricature version of a European farewell, with a kiss on each cheek. At least it left me laughing...instead of crying, which some girls may have been doing about four minutes into this date, just trying to make sense of it all.

I got into my squeaky-clean car, still laughing at the first-rate entertainment that had just ensued, wishing I had recorded the entire adventure. I couldn't get home fast enough so that I could drop in on Rebecca, who set us up in the first place. But what would I tell her? Nice, yes. Kind, yes. Smart...brilliant in fact. Hilarious to the point where my stomach hurt from laughing so hard. But the whole date was a stand-up comic routine. And I don't think it was just nerves ~ I'm pretty certain that was his comfort zone that he hovers in most of the time. I can't imagine how utterly boring I must have seemed to him.

As catastrophic as it may sound in terms of a first date, I must say that I certainly appreciated the constant flow of laughter from start to finish, which definitely beats sitting at home alone, surfing through Netflix over and over again. There's nothing like a date with Marcus to awaken the senses. Sensational, yet gently terrifying, since I never knew what was coming at me next. What a dichotomy of emotions vibrating simultaneously throughout my body.

Honestly? I think everyone should experience a Marcus once in a lifetime. It really does make you re-examine the idle 78% of your personality that maybe could do with a bit of dusting off now and then.

From: Sophie
To: Rebecca
Subject: **Epic...!**
Sent: Saturday, April 11 4:39 pm

Hey Rebecca,

I dropped by your place today on my way home from my date with Marcus since I had an urgent need to debrief...! Did you mention anything to me about his wild side? His really, really wild side? I feel sorry for the other bachelors to follow since I laughed the whole time with Marcus. But sorry to say (as I am sure you are busting to know)...I don't think we are meant to be a match made in heaven. But that's O.K.!

He has certainly expanded my horizons and made me realize what is out there – I definitely have been leading a *very* sheltered life, apparently!

I have Date #3 coming up soon with Coach Jake. That will put me beyond the half-way point to my debriefing party. Can't wait!!

Hope the Easter Bunny is good to you tomorrow :)
Sophie

From: Rebecca
To: Sophie
Subject: **Re: Epic...!**
Date: Sunday, April 12 5:50 am

Hey! Glad you had a good time! I think I mentioned that he has a great sense of humour and that he is larger than life...but, I really, really want to know about his wild side! Do tell!

On to the next!

Have a great week ahead.

Rebecca

From: Hockey - Coach Jake
To: Sophie
Subject: Out for a Drink
Date: Sunday, April 12   10:07 am

Hey Sophie,

Hope you're having a great Easter weekend. I ate too much but that's what happens when I go home to family.

We have to get together to add up your dates. I know you said Wednesdays are good for you but I am starting my soccer training this week on Wednesday nights. This week is going to be a bit busy but I will call you and we can try and figure something out...?

Jake

From: Sophie
To: Hockey - Coach Jake
Subject: Re: Out for a Drink
Date: Monday, April 13   10:52 am

Hi Jake,

We had a really good weekend, too - I somehow controlled

myself, despite the amount of chocolate that came through the door. It is added to the stash I still have left over from Valentine's Day and Christmas. (A "when in doubt, give your teacher chocolate" thing.)

I forgot about your soccer on Wednesday nights. That night is always a guarantee for me but I usually have flexibility. Look at your schedule and let's see what we can work out.

You wanted to be my first, but at this rate you'll end up being my last!

From: Hockey - Coach Jake
To: Sophie
Subject: **Re: Out for a Drink**
Date: Monday, April 13 11:54 am

Sophie,

I hope you share the chocolate. I have a thing for it in any shape or form. Ah, yes - I may be the last, but I promise to be the best ;)

As soon as my soccer calendar comes out, I'll know the times a little better. I will keep you posted but I look forward to having a refreshment.

From: Sophie
To: Hockey - Coach Jake
Subject: best date
Date: Monday, April 13 2:03 pm

Of course I share. That's what I do for a living - I teach sharing. I have the stash near the door and give it out to whoever will take it off my hands (and therefore away from my hips) when they're leaving. (Except, of course, when Cameron intercepts :)

The spot for "best date" is still available (unfortunately for me). "Most Memorable", however, has been taken and secured. To be honest, I think I am still experiencing shell-shock from it! He was a really great guy, but I couldn't keep up with his sense of humour and wild antics. Picture Robin Williams and Richard Prior herding cats.

Did I tell you that part of setting this goal meant that I had to set a reward for myself for enduring this craziness? So, my reward is a party with 5 girlfriends to debrief the 5 dates.

Except, now everybody wants to come. Including Bachelor # 2. He thinks that I should invite the top 3 bachelors to the party and then have all of my girlfriends vote on who they like best.

Maybe not a bad idea...?

Sophie

From: Hockey - Coach Jake
To: Sophie
Subject: Re: best date
Date: Sunday, April 12   2:42 pm

I think it's a great reward...but this bachelor suggests you reward yourself with a trip down south and the 5 girls can join you. Forget the 5 bachelors up here. Go for bachelors in bathing suits!

Boy-oh-boy...I'd better get a move on it. The boys sure are lining up. Great reason for it, though. I'm looking forward to seeing you outside of the cold hockey rink for a change.

~

Sitting beside me in a dark, half-empty movie theatre was Cameron, loving every minute of Monsters vs. Aliens. It was Easter Sunday and all I kept thinking was just how sacrilegious this whole scenario must have appeared. My grandfather – a former Presbyterian minister – would be rolling over in his grave if he knew that this is how I was spending such a religious day with my son.

Reese Witherspoon was playing a freakishly tall animated character who had a classic Oprah aha moment when she realized that her fiancé was a complete jerk.

I pulled out my phone in the dark movie theatre and typed out her words - directly from the movie – into an e-mail to myself:

From: Sophie
To: Home
Subject: Never again
Date: Sunday, April 12 4:56 pm

"I am never going to short-change myself ever again."

Her words had to become my words. I naively chose the wrong man for a lifelong marriage ~ as lovely as he was; and then foolishly chose a very wrong man to date. I'd moved the line in the sand too many times, nudging it further and further back. For no explicable reason.

But no more. Enough of Mr. Good Enough. I had to take the bull by the horns, set definitive guidelines and standards that *would be* written in stone. A new day had come and I liked how it felt ~ like there was no looking back…no turning back. This was the moment I realized that I had reached the point of no return.

Three Questions

I foolishly somehow completely forgot to call Charlotte after my date with William on Friday. She must have been chomping at the bit, wondering how her match-making skills had stacked up in the end.

I called her the moment I remembered on Sunday evening, allowing the opportunity to fill her in on not one, but two dates. Charlotte is one of the funniest people I know, largely due to the fact that she is one of the smartest people I know, with a PhD in chemistry to boot.

After a marathon of laughter, she followed up with an e-mail, which had become the norm with this dating project of mine. I think that it caused so much curiosity and reflection which then continued even after my girlfriends and I finished chatting with each other. It seems that people just can't get enough of this concept of putting a goal out there and actively getting your entire support network to help you reach that goal. It's like everyone had intuitively made it their personal responsibility to catapult me across the finish line.

From: Charlotte

To: Sophie

Subject: 3 questions

Date: Sunday, April 12   10:57 pm

Hi there,

Gosh, it was fun to finally catch up tonight – kind of like Girls' Night Out without ever leaving the house. Easy!

Sophie, I know I've said this before, but I have to tell you again that you are incredibly brave to be doing all of this. Most people can hardly handle the idea of one blind date, let alone 5. And all self-inflicted at that! Wow. It is so much easier being the outsider looking in.

I don't think the rules of dating at our age should be much different than the ones my nieces have to observe. Anyone who is talking about sex in the first 20 minutes had better be "the one" or be willing to be cast aside.

My nieces allow their mom to ask 3 questions of a potential boyfriend when he comes to the house on a first date. It's mostly stuff like: where do you work...what do you do for your employer...do you have a hobby.

I looked at the model and tried to build a better set of questions for you. For instance:
* Are there any restraining orders from previous girlfriends?
* Are there any children floating around out there who might be biologically related to you?

OK, so I kid. (Sort of.)

But if you meet someone through this whole process who you might want to move forward with, I guess I'd like to ask him these 3 questions:

1) Will you treat my good friend so well that you can look me in the eye and guarantee me that she's OK, every time I ask you?

This question I ask for Sophie, to know if you can be my good friend, even though we've never met.

2) Will you treat her son and former husband with kindness, fairness and dignity?

As I see it, a family that split up was not a family that failed, in this case – just a family that was led by adults who saw a better path for everyone involved.

This question I ask for Cameron and Nick, who are good friends of mine for good reason. They've challenged me to look at myself with an honest perspective, and I've made some less selfish decisions because of their opinions. They are both good people.

3) Will you give Sophie equal voice and footing in this relationship, regardless of things like money, beauty, gender, job status, health, political leanings, religion and a seemingly ridiculous choice of an NHL team?

This question I ask because I have an interest in all women, and I believe that Sophie has as well.

Sophie – keep me posted. If I need to buy a dress for an event, I need a timeline!

Signed,

Charlotte…. your de facto older brother

From: Sophie
To: Julia
Subject: Withdrawal
Sent: Tuesday, April 14 3:57 pm

Hey sweets,

I have not had an e-mail from anyone - not even junk mail - all day. After going 10 straight days with *constant* e-mails, I am going through official withdrawal. Seriously! Help me!

Could you at least hit reply - even if it's just a blank screen? I just need to hear that addictive fairy dust sound when an e-mail gets delivered.

Signed,
Pathetic but true...

From: Julia
To: Sophie
Subject: Re: Withdrawal
Date: Tuesday, April 14 4:09 pm

I'm here for you, girl!

Do you want me to send you some of my work to do??? That'll keep you distracted ;)

J

From: Julia

To: Sophie

Cc: Diana

Subject: **Fwd: date?**

Date: Thursday, April 17 11:59 am

Hey Soph,

Great news! Read the e-mail from Diana below. A bright spot on a grey day :)

Morning Julia :)

Can you please pass on Sophie's e-mail address to me? I've got a date lined up for her – a guy I met who actually lives in Applecross. (How convenient!)

It's one thing to read about her dating endeavour, but a whole different universe to be a part of it. What a rush, and I'm not even the one who will be going on the date!

Diana

From: Diana
To: Sophie
Subject: **Re: date?**
Date: Thursday, April 17 4:37 pm

Sophie!

Exciting news! Do you remember the guy I mentioned to you about a couple weeks ago at Julia's house? I ran into him again and so I bridged the topic of his marital status (that was fun ;) and it turns out he's single. He's also open to a coffee date. I don't know him very well, but he assured me he's not a serial killer (phew!), so, if you're game, I will connect the two of you.

FYI – His name is Calvin and he's 37 years old. He owns his own contracting business and is also a real estate investor. He owns a home in Applecross and an additional home up north in the Muskoka's. He seems very honest and nice...but I really don't know much more. I don't have him as a friend on Facebook, but I noticed he does have a profile if you want to check him out.

Oh - BTW – you do know that Diana was the Greek Goddess of the Hunt, right? (OK, technically Roman, but Greek makes me sound way more exotic.) That makes me hand-picked to help you in your quest to find Mr. Right ;) The stars are aligning in your favour, Sophie ~ I can feel it!

I'll connect you when you're ready.......

Diana

P.S. Just curious... how have your dates gone thus far? Since I've been married to my husband for a zillion years...what would you say the challenge is?

From: Sophie
To: Diana
Subject: Too many to count!
Sent: Monday, April 20 8:14 pm

Hey there,

I re-read your e-mail and noticed that "challenge" was singular. Alert the media! There are many!!! And mustering up the courage to write/speak/meet is not one of them for me. Imagine what it is like for people who are shy!

Here goes:

1) ...Finding the right thing to wear – big (...as incredibly shallow as that sounds...) Think about it - that first impression is powerful and permanent.

2) ...Having chemistry with someone by e-mail and then not in person...very disappointing. But, then, the hard part is finding the emotional energy to start up again with someone else, after you thought something would come of the last one who turned out to be a shocker.

3) ...Being on a date, knowing they like you and want to see you again, but you know that you have to find a way to let them down gently.

4) ...Wondering how to tell the person who set you up that you aren't interested (...I hate to disappoint people, especially friends), knowing that there is NO WAY that the mutual friend has seen the side of your blind date that blocks the compatibility...hence, afraid your cupid won't understand.

There are good things, though, for sure, with the best part being what you learn from the experience - how not to behave/dress/worry...

Missing this stage in your life? Don't!!! I can't wait to be out of it!

To be honest...I'm not looking for someone to go out with. I just want to find a man to stay home with.

S

From: Diana
To: Sophie
Subject: **Ahhh...I get it!**
Date: Monday, April 20 9:33 pm

I agree...! And I apologize for my simplification. I so get it. You're looking for a connection. A heart, head and reality-based connection.

Within the goal to not be single, do you know what you really want? Or, rather, what you do *not* want? I always loved the chase and the excitement, but if I was to do it today in this day-and-age, I think I would have to have a much larger picture in my approach. A pickier picture, too, because chemistry isn't everything, nor is friendship, is it? Ideally, a combination. I think, as a woman at my age, I can be clear about identifying what I will - or will not - accept within my world. Oh, the fun of living in fantasy!

I have NO expectations around your date with Calvin. He is personable and has a lovely smile that is warm and caring. He is a combination – a man paired with a confidence in revealing his more sensitive side, I think. You will know a lot more once you get together, but if he's none of those things, then you can kick him to the curb with no worries ;) I wish I could be a fly on the wall!

Hmmm...what to wear. From the few times I've seen him – go casual. He's not a business suit or even dressy-casual guy. More of a jeans guy. He's originally from up north so I assume that he's pretty down to earth...?

Just be beautiful you. I really think you deserve to share your life with someone who appreciates you.

I'm rambling, but the next question is...why are so many women in the same spot as you? I have 4 or 5 amazing girlfriends – smart, attractive...great personalities - all looking and wanting the same thing. There is obviously an availability gap in the world of dating!

From: Diana
To: Sophie; Calvin
Subject: Coffee & Conversation
Date: Monday, April 20 11:51 pm

Dear Calvin and Sophie,

It's my pleasure to virtually introduce the two of you. I know only a limited amount about both of you, but from what I do know, I feel confident in saying that you are both sincere, likable and good looking! I'll leave the rest up to you :)

Sophie - please meet Calvin. Calvin...Sophie.

Enjoy the date and meeting someone new.

Cheers,
Diana

From: Calvin
To: Diana; Sophie
Subject: Re: Coffee & Conversation
Date: Tuesday, April 21 9:19 am

Ladies,

What an introduction! I've never seen it done quite like that before, but I like it.

Thanks, Diana, for the compliments, especially for considering me worthy of meeting Sophie.

Sophie - Diana was full of compliments of you in her brief description when we spoke recently. So, if you would like to e-mail me sometime or chat, the invitation is open.

Regards,
Calvin

Get a Life! (...no offence)

From: Sophie
To: Julia
Subject: **Spread it around?**
Sent: Wednesday, April 22   10:57 pm

Hey, you!

I would have loved to have been at your workshop today, but unfortunately the reality of work got in the way, yet again. I think it is great that you took Abby – hardly your baby girl anymore, is she? I am sure she was bursting with pride to see her mama bear standing up there, shining like a superstar.

That goal-setting workshop that you did with Rebecca and me – do you think I could get a copy of the questions that you ran us through?

I am mildly considering trying it on a few people myself. A bunch of colleagues have been hanging off my every word, looking for daily updates on my **5 Dates** plan. Even my Vice Principal, who is normally soooooo quiet, has gotten in on the action, elbowing for a spot at my lunch table. It's been unbelievable.

To be honest, I am almost getting sick of hearing my own stories. That's how intense the interest is - throughout my world, actually - not just at work. I finally said at work today that anyone who wants to sit with me at lunch needs to bring more to the table (no pun intended) – they must start setting their own goals. (Anything to spice up the conversation!) But here's the thing – I was only half joking. Now that my life is more interesting, I kinda want the same in others. (Is that normal??)

Moi

From: Julia
To: Sophie
Subject: **Re: Spread it around?**
Date: Thursday, April 23   6:44 am
Attachment: Getting Your Life on a Roll.doc

Of course – great idea! Go for it! (Attached.)

Have fun with it ~

Julia

The Greek God

I walked up to the café, tucked into a gorgeous little spot overlooking the river, to find my bachelor waiting for me outside on the patio. It was later in April now and the weather had finally warmed up, allowing for vibrant patio umbrellas to pop up at every available outdoor venue. I could tell it was Calvin by the way his eyes followed me from my car, and by the smile that gradually continued to grow on his face.

You seem...he said, as our handshake was still fresh.

...Rushed?

Yes – rushed.

You're right. I'm sorry - not a good first impression for a blind date.

It was a bizarre experience getting ready for today's escapade. What complicated it all was the fact that, right after this coffee date with Calvin, I was headed to an indoor rink to watch some of my students in a skating show. I had to look professional for my students and their parents, which didn't match the protocol for a first date with a total stranger. On top of the decision of what look to go with, I was warned to come prepared to sit in an especially cold rink.

I guess the pressure of professionalism trumped the date card since I arrived to meet Calvin dressed in an outfit that looked a little too formal. Bursting with spring colours, yes, but definitely a very 'proper' look instead of a warm first impression. I could tell as soon as I got out of the car that I had made the wrong wardrobe choice and spent the ten second walk to greet **Bachelor # 3** wishing I could rewind the clock and completely edit my outfit.

We naturally gravitated to the obvious topics of a first date. He was a contractor-turned-real estate agent, floating back and forth between the two occupations. All I kept thinking was how perfect he could make my home, neglected due to my dreadful handyman skills. Think...gorgeous granite counter tops. Think…skylights in every room. That's it. The jury had reached a verdict. Clearly, I had to make this work.

But there it was. Sports. Hobbies. Schooling. Careers. Family. Done. The whole gamut...all within a total of eight minutes.

This never happens to me. Ever. I can usually make conversation with anyone. ANYONE. I do it with complete strangers all the time. I once had a seven-hour non-stop conversation with a man who sat next to me on that marathon flight from L.A. to Sydney. I had the novel Pompeii tucked in the seat pocket in front of me and it just so happens that he did his PhD thesis in archaeology. At Pompeii. We barely stopped to take a breath the entire time, but our heads finally collapsed back into our seats when we were desperate for some long overdue shut-eye.

And, here I was, only on my third of 5 dates, running out of ways to keep it alive. This was not a good sign. Had I seriously lost my groove already? But we essentially had nothing in common. Both smart, happy people interested in life. Just not interested in each other.

He was a Greek god – a vision to behold with his muscular-but-not-too-muscular chest. (Obviously, from all those years of lugging around granite counter tops.) How could I pass this up? Talented. Funny. Nice as hell. Gorgeous. And yet I couldn't wait to leave. I'm sure he felt the same.

I remember saying good-bye to him in the parking lot, and I remember the vision that was in my head at the time – squeezing both of his perfect biceps simultaneously – firmly, but affectionately. But, as impossible as this may sound, I honestly don't know if that was just a visual fantasy rolling around in my head, or if this memory actually took place. (The rambling on my part did occur; that I know. An exit as impressive as my entry. Lovely.)

Regardless, the caressing of his biceps still lingers with sweetness in my mind, like the taste of vanilla ice cream on a hot summer's day. Oh, the magnetic power of physical attraction. Just not powerful enough this time. I guess Cupid's arrow was slightly amiss ~ a wee bit out of practice, it seems.

We said our good-byes and parted ways, both of us disappointed that there was no need to keep the coffee pot brewing beyond our second handshake.

Losing Steam

Three dates and three weeks into this dating adventure and I was already starting to feel major burn-out. Not a lack of interest. Just...I don't know – a bit emotionally confused. Emotionally overloaded. Granted, Jake was in that mix as well, making it four men that I was keeping track of. Not all at once, of course. Most of it was linear – one after another. Jake was the only constant from the onset of the project.

And there was nothing physical involved – mainly just a simple handshake with each of them. So, why the fading appetite?

What I want to know is how on earth do the players in this world cope? And, the true players are very, very playful, if you know what I mean. I must be missing something in my DNA not to be able to participate in their league. I'm so emotionally unqualified to be a player that there's no way that I would even be let in the front door of their clubhouse. I wouldn't even be allowed in the parking lot.

But I am starting to wonder if the players are the ones missing something in *their* DNA that they can lead the life of constantly switching love interests. Regardless, this was clearly outside of my comfort zone. (I guess this is the point in the show when The Bachelors and Bachelorettes complain about how gruelling life is and expect us to feel sorry for them while they are being swept off to Paris and Thailand.) (Except, I'm not even venturing 20 km from home! Note to self: Next dating project must include international flights.)

I had to take a bit of a break - a pause, we'll call it – just to catch my breath a bit, long enough to keep me out of therapy.

Some mild banter with Jake continued back and forth over the next ten days or so, but that was it. Light and fun…just enough to keep my dating pulse alive.

In contrast to my fizzle, I was getting word back from my cupids that the men were really charged by the whole concept of it all. Knowing that they would be one of five really brought out the alpha male in each of them ~ including William, who was not even going to be living in the same hemisphere…! Animal nature, at its best. I love it.

The Things People Say!

Not only does the month of May bring the much-craved warmth to our little nook of the planet, it also marks the opening of our local farmers' market.

It is held outdoors on a local side street that is easy to close off to vehicles. It also sits directly in front of the 100-year-old elementary school that I attended as a child, making it even that much more charming and special to me.

I love the whole market experience for many reasons – the fabulous aromas, the fresh local produce, the artisans whose talents amaze me each and every Saturday...

Ahhh ~ then there is my favourite Frenchman who produces the most delectable crêpes, right before your eyes, and makes you feel like you are in the heart of magnificent Paris. It is always hard to choose between the strawberry crêpe, oozing with melted Nutella, or the peach one with a salty caramel sauce drizzled throughout.

I love it that Pierre single-handedly brings that unique European flare to our little town gathering. He hails from Normandy which is where the 1882 design of my family home originates from. This was the only connection we needed to solidify a friendship that is renewed every Saturday morning throughout the warm summer months. Furthermore, all of the French Immersion kids – including my own – get a rare practical opportunity to use the French that they speak all day at school before switching to English once they get home.

It was on my way to his mouth-watering stall, passing by the floral section at the front of the market, when I heard the words that literally stopped me in my tracks in disbelief:

After my second marriage, said a fashionable slender woman under her broad brimmed hat.

Wait, said her bewildered listener, **Did you have *two* marriages??**

Of course I did! They're ALL disposable, you know!

I did such a sudden double-take that I nearly ended up at the chiropractor's office later that day. Clearly, I don't get out much if these are the new rules floating around out there! I was really starting to believe that I just didn't have enough life experience for this brand-new era of boy-meets-girl. The timing of my slight hiatus could not have come at a better time. I definitely needed to come up for air, tread water and just enjoy the scenery a bit before it was safe to go back into the water again.

Busy & Butchered

When I finally did regain my emotional energy to dive back in with the boys, Jake was ready. His hectic work schedule of jetting back and forth to New York had settled down a bit. **Pick a date**, his e-mail said.

When I called him to try to coordinate our schedules, he was shocked when I presented my suggestion of May 15th. **But that was ten days away**, he pointed out with an almost wounded confusion.

It had taken him four weeks to finally make time for our date – this, despite his request of **Can I be the first?** Could he not see the hypocrisy in his shock and disappointment that now he was the one having to wait? I wonder if he thought I was punishing him for taking so long for our rendezvous.

But there was not an ounce of any cerebral competition being played here, I swear. Trust me – I was bursting at the seams to materialize our long-awaited first date. But, I, too, was busy.

Busy, and chopped up, that is.

Busy, with a huge work assignment. I had been invited to do some prestigious curriculum writing about a year ago and it was coming to a climax with a presentation to the head of the school board. I was the chief presenter and so this was big for me ~ literally the biggest moment of my career, and it required several preparation meetings and multiple late nights at work.

The chopped-up bit, not so glamorous. It all started several months ago when Cameron and I were at the tail end of a trip to Australia. It was wonderful ~ the first time we had been back since leaving my son's home and native land eight years ago. Back in the day, when I was a married woman, we moved to Australia when I was eight months pregnant. So pregnant, that I looked and felt like I was ready to burst at any given moment. Despite what most people assume to this day, it was actually my idea to move Down Under at a time in my life when most women are busy nesting and getting their feet massaged. Insanity, I know, especially given my tight bond with my family. How could I have possibly left my mother at the most crucial time in my life? Even in hindsight, I have no idea how I did it.

When you have your own child,

you'll realize how much we love you.

Those were my mother's last words to me at the airport as we were parting to move to the other corner of the world. Not just any corner - the far bottom corner. Australia was so far away from home – you couldn't *get* any further away. With a twelve-hour time difference, any further and you'd be on your way back to Canada.

How she had the strength to let me go is still an absolute mystery to me. But it was rock-solid proof that my parents are the most selfless people on the planet. Most people strive for it, but my parents really did succeed at giving us roots for stability and wings to help us fly. And they did it all without a learner's manual ~ proof of the radiant, magical wonder of evolution in full bloom.

So, we set up house in the magnificent Land of Oz, giving our baby boy the amazing good fortune of Australian citizenship. To this day, I think he actually considers himself Australian first. Which I love. But that is despite the fact that he was only two and a bit when we left Australia to be closer to family. He was at such an adorable age, exploring every angle of life with such passion and curiosity. At the time, I thought that the return to Canada was so that my child and my parents would know each other. But, with further reflection, I realize that the move back had more selfish grounds: I wanted the memory of my parents and my child together, involved and interacting in each other's lives. I wanted that video to be able to play in my head for the rest of my life. It was as simple as that. Granted, Cameron was a massive bundle of energy, and having family support to help manage some of that liveliness didn't hurt, either. But there are few things more beautiful than seeing that special and unique bond between your parents and your child.

So, during that trip of a lifetime back to Australia to show Cameron his roots, on our last night in Sydney, I noticed a distinctive red ring around an otherwise harmless freckle on my left leg.

Upon returning home from our spectacular vacation, I saw my doctor pretty much before seeing any friends or family, despite being away for a good chunk of the summer. **Let's wait and see,** he said. Trust me ~ I tried every angle to get him to refer me to a specialist. My uncle had melanoma, twice. My classic Anglo-Saxon fair skin. Blistering sunburns throughout my childhood. But, nothing worked. I couldn't get even the slightest budge out of him.

I kept going. **You know how long it takes to get a specialist appointment these days, right? Well, how about we book it and then I will cancel it if the mole clears up?** It was at that point that he realized that I was not giving up. I simply was not leaving his office without that referral ~ the only golden ticket that could restore my suspicious peace of mind.

Two weeks later, the dermatologist took a good look and said, **I don't know about that one, but I *am* concerned about this one**, as his special little magnifying glass whipped up to my forearm. The lab reports for both of them came back as pre-cancerous. Left untreated, I was told, and they both would have turned into melanoma. That die-hard persistence that is both my strength and my weakness? Well, it turns out it may have actually saved my life this time.

I was quickly transferred under the care of a plastic surgeon who would be able to cut deeper than what the dermatologist was able to perform in his office. Now, deeper sounds harsh, but it wasn't, really – we're talking the difference of maybe a few millimetres, at most. But it is obviously a key difference when it comes to problematic freckles.

Over the next eight months, I was frequently in and out of the day surgery section of the hospital. It seemed that every time I went to get the results from my last procedure, my specialist would be curious about another freckle on another part of my body. In that block of time, nine freckles were removed. Three of them were pre-cancerous. The specialist reminded me again: left untreated and they would have turned into not just cancer, but melanoma. Ouch.

It was a screaming example of not letting up when listening to my instincts ~ like a dog on a bone. I was just shy of getting down on my hands and knees to get the proper attention for my questionable spots. What scares me the most is the fact that likely 90% of patients would have accepted my G.P.'s original dismissal. How many people are out there walking around as ticking time bombs? All because they did not pay attention to the red flags or, worse, didn't stand up for their own health when their doctor didn't take them seriously. I'm sure the actual figure would be staggering.

So, here I was, finally getting the green light from Jake, and I was cut up and stitched up, this time in three different places. I looked and felt like Frankenstein and I just couldn't get that identity out of my head. I had waited too long for this moment with Jake and I was not prepared to finally go out with him feeling so...so butchered.

May 15th it would have to be, allowing me enough time to shed my sewn-up look and be stitches-free.

But one thing made it all worthwhile ~ all the slicing and dicing that I hated with a passion:

From: Danielle
To: Sophie
Subject: Close call
Date: Thursday, May 7 8:32 am

Sophie,

Sometimes we share tips and personal stories with our girlfriends. And sometimes – but not always - we pay attention to each other's tips and personal stories.

I listened nonchalantly to your 'battle of the blades' – how you had a hunch about a freckle and how you almost had to kick and scream to be taken seriously.

I quietly noticed over time some changes happening on my right arm – some itching and a bit of bleeding. I heard your voice in my head over and over again, retelling the details of your own account.

Because of you, sharing your story, I took action. It was not only a problem: it was melanoma.

I don't want any sympathy. (I'm serious, girl.) Just tell this story to anyone and everyone who will listen.

You saved my life, girlfriend. That's big.

Danielle

Life doesn't get any better than that.

Mr. Starbucks

Despite being swamped at work over the next several dateless days that followed, I couldn't stop thinking about Jake. But I did have the overall 5 Dates objective to keep in mind as well. And I am very much one who does what I am told. That is why goal-setting is so powerful for me. A goal with a list of clear steps and guidelines to follow, written on hardcopy paper, is, for me, an obligation ~ a set of strict instructions. It's equivalent to a binding contract that I must abide by.

With the ten-day wait evaporating, I realized that Jake was going to be Date # 4. And there was something just not fitting about that ~ it didn't have the right ring to it. I didn't like the idea of him being crammed somewhere in the middle of the grand total of five. But the reality was that it was out of my control as I had no other offers coming in.

Until...one fell out of the sky onto my lap. Actually ~ onto Julia's lap. But he still came out of nowhere, even to her. She was quietly working away on her computer at Starbucks one uneventful afternoon, as she typically does on any given day of the week. It is her second home. She buys her chai tea latté, maybe an oatmeal chocolate square ~ melted just so, then hunkers down on her computer to perform her best work of the day. There's something about all of the hustle and bustle in the background - almost like the white noise phenomenon - that allows her to dive in and settle into just the right zone. Regardless of the rationale, it works like a charm for her.

Those are some rocks you've got there.

Hmmm...?? Julia looked around, peering over top of her

reading glasses with sudden confusion.

The rocks on your finger - are they real? And I do mean 'rocks'.

Julia twisted her neck around and realized that the stranger's voice was coming from the handsome gentleman peering over her shoulder. Happily married, but always a good sport, she joined in on this playful game of flirtatious ping-pong.

Sorry to disappoint, but, yes – they are very real.

With a very real husband to go along with them?

Sorry again, she said with the most gorgeous glow in town. **I *am* married. Very married, in fact.** She just sat there, staring with a lingering smile for what counts as a millennium in my books, before she suddenly snapped out of her fantasy world and realized, **But – hey! I have a friend who is single!** And with those words, she simultaneously stood up and shook his hand, with a very inconspicuous yet specific motive in mind.

Let me complete the picture about Julia and me. She is a master influencer with her career in corporate behavioural change. And let me tell you – she is a consummate expert in this field of persuasion, with me as living proof. You see, any and every suggestion she has ever given me, I have followed. To the letter. Contrary to how this must sound, I'm not spineless by any means ~ just always open to any available perspective. And Julia always has a perspective. In a good way. Quite like Oprah – out to help everyone lead their best life. And with me being single, there is space in my life for someone to come in to make suggestions. Had I not been single, that opening would likely be filled by my spouse. And given the amount of time we spend together (thanks to her husband's dedication to their home reno), of course she would be the one to fill that role. Picture something like a rare combination of sisters, BFF's and spouses, all morphed into one unique relationship bundle.

But there was one time when I didn't take her advice, and let's just say, she was not impressed. Not from a control perspective, but merely because she just could not, for the life of her, comprehend my reasoning.

It was about a year ago. She had heard of a single guy who was a friend of a friend's and she thought it would be a great idea for me to go out with him on a blind date. The fact that he was a stranger was not the issue for me. But the gentleman was...and dare I admit my shallowness...shorter than I am. By a good inch. Which really meant three inches most of the time when in my every day shoes...four, when I put on my fancy party shoes.

I tried. I really, really tried to get around my pathetic hang-up of what should be completely inconsequential. And I admire ~ no, I am downright *jealous* of the women who have no issues with a shorter man. Trust me - I wanted to be like Nicole Kidman and Tina Fey who rock the whole 'taller than their man' thing. But I just couldn't do it. My loss, for sure.

And, I would think that Julia, of all people would understand. Her first husband was a tall one at 6'2". But Tim – Tim is a massive 6'7" – an entire foot taller than she is!

Thankfully, our friendship recovered. She still doesn't understand my pickiness in the height department but at least she respects it. Which is why she deliberately stood up while talking to Mr. Starbucks. It turns out he was a few inches taller, easily making the cut. Little did he know that he was about to become **Bachelor # 4**.

~

Julia caught me, by chance, lingering in my parents' doorway later that day. Living a few doors down from them, she often passes their house while out for a lazy after-dinner walk with her kids. It is such a beautiful neighbourhood with huge old maple trees providing much-welcomed shade to the majestic Victorian homes. Consequently, strolling is a common past-time for many of the locals.

She rushed over at the sight of me and we somehow managed to have a full conversation about Mr. Starbucks. All, completely in coded conversation to keep it private from not only our kids, but also from my parents. (Definitely too much information for them.)

She pulled out her phone and produced a photo of him with his two kids that he had e-mailed to her, and there we were, oooh-ing over it like two teenage girls. He was definitely handsome, and his kids looked...I don't know. I'd say...well-behaved…? Impossible to tell from a photo, I know. But they did. They looked like they were good kids. I was all in! Why not?!

With it being Monday evening, it meant that my date with Jake was a mere three days away. Jake wanted to be my first, but since he couldn't be the gold standard for all the others to be compared to, I really wanted him to be my last.

That meant some expert juggling in order to squeeze in this newly discovered single man ASAP. It was tricky, but I have never been one to let obstacles get in the way of anything important. And this was important. We plotted for Cameron to go to Julia's house on Tuesday after school. That would allow him to play with her kids and it would free me up to see if **Bachelor # 4** – David - was, in fact, the future Mr. Right.

Thanks to being independently wealthy, David had total flexibility in his schedule. We met at 4:30 pm at the same Starbucks where Julia first met him. He was about my height, very fit and surprisingly as handsome as his photo. So far so good. I wasn't used to the slicked-back hair look, but it was all definitely worth a go.

He warned me ahead of time that he was expecting a call from his son so they could coordinate a pick-up time in a couple of hours. There was a definite difference with this scenario from Bachelor # 1. Marcus left his phone on the café table and read and replied to dozens of text messages. David, on the other hand, gave me a heads-up about a particular call that would be coming in from his son. With both of us being parents, there was no need to provide any more details. Kids always come first. Not a problem.

I was definitely pleased with Bachelor # 4. I'd say our date was going along just fine, with a smooth transition from topic to topic. I could completely understand why Julia selected him for the coveted final opening on my dance card. He was smart, articulate, successful in business, attractive. Who could complain about any of that?! In fact, I was so comfortable that I was almost a bit worried for Jake's sake. This date was starting to look like a tough act to follow.

The expected interruption came in about half way into our date. He looked at the number on call display and took the call with a smile on his face and a polite nod towards me. But the smile instantly snapped into a very different face – a face that was hostile and intimidating. His tone mirrored his look. Much to his surprise, it was his ex-wife. My only guess is that David's son was expected to call from his mom's house, hence David accepting the call from that number with pleasant expectations.

What I witnessed was, in a nutshell, disturbing. His demeanour and words quickly became abrupt, dismissive and downright ugly. I decided to give him the complete benefit of the doubt – that it was all his ex-wife's fault for mustering such a strong, negative reaction from David. Let's assume that she *was* a vindictive and manipulative person. A nightmare. And let's assume that David is normally heaven-sent with everyone else in his life. I should keep going and give this a second chance, right?

But, twice before in my life, I had ignored the warning signs with men. Once, with the man I had married. Then, again, with the next man I let into in my life - just like today, in this moment with David – the hairs raised up on the back of my neck on a first date, screaming to get my attention. And I remember thinking, during the mountain of horrific struggles that ensued with the latter: Why didn't I flee at the first sign of trouble? All his other women did. Why didn't I?

In the case with both men, it was an example of my perseverance being my own worst enemy: **They can change! (...if I just work hard enough.)** My ex-husband really didn't need to change – he just needed a better match as we evolved in different directions. The other guy? Definitely. But I now realize that it was not my responsibility in life to get him the medical attention that he so desperately needed, yet vehemently refused. My next New Year's resolution? Know when to walk away from a train wreck.

Even if David turned out to be all saintly and sweet, I did not have any room in my life for a complicated ex-wife. More importantly, I had no room in my life if David turned out to be the antagonistic and problematic one in this tête-à-tête that was playing out before my eyes. Regardless of who was to blame, I had no room in my life for tantrums or control issues from anyone, for that matter. Experience has taught me the hard way that being alone is a lot less lonely than being in a relationship full of chaos and drama.

I instantly checked out of our date. I remained sitting across from him, of course, but in body only. I couldn't ignore the raised hairs on the back of my neck any longer. In the past, each warning signal my body sent me was snuffed out as quickly and easily as the flame of a candle. With one fell swoop: extinguished...dismissed. I'd been treating my instincts throughout my life as if they were more of a malfunction rather than the survival tool that they truly are. I'd be damned if I was going to make the same mistake again. I simply had to stop ignoring the red flags that were being waved aggressively, directly in my face, time and time again. I had finally learned my lesson. I had to trust my instincts this time around.

And, funny. What an immensely empowering and unexpected feeling it turned out to be. And really, what was so hard about it? Nothing. Nothing at all. In fact, it took a lot less energy to go with my gut instead of fighting against it, as I had too many times before in my life. Note to self: Oprah was right ~ trust my gut.

I did my best to make chitchat, trying not to let on that all I wanted was to turn around and disappear for good. He had tickets to go see the upcoming Billy Joel and Elton John concert. Did I want to go? I urged him, **You should take your son. He would love it!** But his son was not interested. Nor his daughter.

Stress had set in as soon as I saw that dark side of him earlier in the date. As a result, my mind was clouded and focused on my exit strategy and so the rest of the details of the date are a complete blur. But I do know that I somehow managed to make the necessary small talk and I somehow was able to end the date politely without leading him on. He was aware that, at the end of the date, he unfortunately still had a spare ticket to that sold-out concert.

There was a definite chance that I was making a mistake, that I was passing up on a chance at true love. But my past was whispering. My heart had previously been guilty of getting drunk with lust and infatuation too quickly, smudging my vision of reality. It's the very reason why I started following the rule of never kissing on a first date. I was normally a risk-taker in life, but after a mismatched marriage and a horrific second act, I had to play it safe: I had to err on the side of caution and move on from **Bachelor # 4**.

~

The best part of the evening was pulling into Julia's driveway, breezing in through the front door and melting into my chair at the over-sized dining room table to the gastronomical delights of a gourmet meal. Nancy, their super-talented nanny, had prepared my favourite: a healthy, oversized version of Thai spring rolls, set next to a delectable green salad bursting with colour. It was like she had a sixth sense and predicted that I would need a soft place to fall tonight. Comfort never felt so warm and secure.

At Last...

The disappointment of how Date # 4 crumbled in such an unpredictable manner, combined with the commotion of the final prep for my curriculum presentation, meant that I hardly gave Jake a moment's thought. I suppose that was a good thing, as I'm sure that I would have spent those next 48 hours obsessing over the details as to how my fifth and final date would unfold.

There was a tickle of a reminder of the approaching rendezvous when a brief e-mail came in on Wednesday afternoon at work, with only one more sleep to go: **Looking forward to tomorrow night. Pick you up at 8?**

It's a good thing my students were outside for lunch recess when I read the message, because I had to talk to someone – ANYONE! Immediately! Poor Mr. Yip got more of an earful than he had bargained for, when really all he wanted was to refill his coffee cup in the nearby staffroom.

Pick me up for our date? Does anyone seriously do that anymore?? Could he be any more stuck in the caveman era??! (Which was more of a statement than a question.)

My normally supportive colleague, who had been married forever, quietly defended Jake: **I think it's kind of...sweet?**

To be perfectly honest, I may have had more superficial concerns than just my independence being squashed here. Like, how would I get in and out of his sports car on my slopped driveway? As trivial as that may sound, picture it. How would it look, me being stuck halfway in and out of his tiny car? More importantly would be the horrific awkwardness of my ex-husband seeing me get dropped off from a date as he looked out my living room window while

Cameron slept upstairs. But my mind was more comfortable skipping straight to the women's lib anthem of **I am woman, hear me roar**.

~

A morning e-mail came in with perfect timing on Thursday, just when my nerves of the day and evening ahead were starting to get the best of me and wear me down:

From: Lucy
To: Sophie
Subject: **Soon?**
Date: Thursday, May 7 8:32 am

Hey,

Don't you have a birthday coming up?? Come by for drinks soon. We'll toast your youth and your beauty!
Lucy

Who needs men when I have friends like that?! This was all I needed to hear to melt away my stress and kick-start my energy for the busy day ahead.

Despite the charming start, the rest of Thursday was a whirlwind. The hours completely flew by as a result of having to teach all day, rush through traffic to get over to the conference centre, appear completely fresh and professional during my presentation to the school board big-wig, whip home to get Cameron set up for Boys' Night with his dad, pop out to the mall for an unsuccessful wardrobe-improvement search, then fall into Julia's arms in her front foyer, with all of the wind knocked out of my sails. **I can't do this – I really, really can't. I don't have an ounce of energy left and I have *NOTHING* to wear.**

Of course you can do this! You've been waiting for this date forever! Hell - *I've* been waiting for this date forever! And, with that, she grabbed me by the hand and dragged me upstairs.

We crossed the threshold of her magnificent walk-in closet and, suddenly, all felt fine. The commotion of the day was completely locked out and it actually seemed soundproof and serene, as if this space was the most perfect spot in the universe. The ultimate oasis. No wonder why Julia is so cheery all the time. Who wouldn't be if you started and ended your day in this incredible space?!

We just stood there at first, surrounded by beautiful clothing and precious jewellery, letting the chaos of the day dissolve from my body. One thing was very clear: I have GOT to spend more time in this closet.

She asked me how I was in the sexy bra department as she opened up a couple of top drawers. Every bra and every set of panties was not only neatly folded, but lined up in the most pristine organized fashion. Oh, the physiological and psychological impact of just the sight of those rows! I can't explain it, but, man, did I feel it. A new standard had been set. I was determined to replicate the same perfection in my own top drawer at home, with row after row of delicate laced beauty.

Bras, panties and skirts, I was fine. (Not that I would actually borrow her panties!) It was the external above-the-waist view that needed attention. We each flipped through our own sections of her closet, eventually covering the entire space from left to right, top to bottom, foraging for the perfect look. We even considered maybe going with a complete dress instead of a skirt and top combo.

We just stood there with blank faces, both of us coming up empty, despite her amazing selection.

What about that? I asked, looking straight at her.

What about what? she asked.

That! This! I said, as I tugged at the dusty-rose coloured top that she was wearing.

Sophie! she said, bursting with laughter. **You can't! It has breast milk on it!**

How is that a problem! That can easily be washed out! And besides - wouldn't that be a secret weapon on a first date? Smelling like his mother during the primal stage of his life? I joked. **I'd have him hook-line-and-sinker in no time!**

By this point, Grace had crawled into the closet and joined us, squirming her way up and onto her mother's hip. I helped Julia pull the top up and over her head towards me, leaving her exposed in her oh-so pretty bra with her breasts plump with milk. Grace couldn't believe her luck. **Bubba?** she asked, as she tapped Julia's left breast, looking for a little pre-dinner snack.

As Julia hugged me good-luck at the door, I squeezed back super tight. **I always knew you loved me enough to give me the shirt off your back in a time of crisis. I guess this is that crisis!**

I drove home with a blended concoction of calmness and excitement running through my veins. Wow. That closet escapade really worked its beautiful magic on me.

I lingered under a nice hot shower, aiming the jets on all of the muscles that typically collect stress. My hair was surprisingly in good shape – the hair gods were apparently working in my corner, thanks to a west wind that blew in at the end of the workday, giving me some extra bounce and body. I savoured this pre-date ritual of beautifying myself, until panic struck when I saw Jake's name coming in on my call display.

Are you ready? He was just checking in.

A quiet Yes was the only response my nerves would allow.

Meet you at 8?

Great – I just have to make one quick stop, but I should be there just shortly after.

I was pleased with my final outfit that I pulled together, piece by piece. A black skirt fell just above the knees, a funky jean jacket allowed Julia's dusty rose top to peak through, and some chunky silver jewellery from Australia topped it all off. It was just right ~ pretty, yet casual without trying too hard.

My 'one quick stop' was popping by to see my very chic and very trendy girlfriend, Emma, who lived just around the corner from me. She had a favourite cropped jacket that she insisted I try on. She wasn't able to contribute a bachelor to my dating project, but a wardrobe contribution would be just as important to her, given her flair for fashion.

Oh! You're wearing a skirt? she asked, as soon as I got out of the car.

Yes...? It's not just coffee – we're doing dinner and drinks. Panic quickly set it. Why? What's wrong?? Tell me what's wrong!

I don't know, Emma wavered. Maybe not? I just thought you'd be wearing pants on your first date with him.

But when else would you wear a skirt? I asked with a calm panic. Skirts were made for first dates, weren't they???

I was utterly confused and completely thrown for a loop. I thought for sure that she would have approved, but I wasn't able to stop and try to figure out the psychology of it all. The ball was about to begin and I definitely didn't have time to go back home to renovate my proverbial gown. I tore off my jean jacket and threw on hers as I ran inside to let the mirror be the judge.

Even if the look had been perfect, there was no way that I could wear it. Her perfume was all over it. I'm no dating expert, but there was no way I was going on this date smelling like another woman.

~

My fifteen-minute drive north seemed like a never-ending eternity. It could have been a shorter journey, had we stuck with the original plan. But, in the few days leading up to tonight, I had mentioned my date to five people, all from completely different walks of life. When they each heard where we were going, all five chimed in, one by one. It was unanimous: **All of the waitresses wear tiny skirts and look like models.** They all insisted: **Switch venues.**

Even Julia agreed. **Listen, girl – I am completely confident in my marriage – you know we're strong and have a great sex life, but even I make sure that we never go there on date night.**

How could I not know this? Some of them mentioned that the food at Milestones would be better as well, so that is what I went with when I suggested to Jake that we go the extra distance.

I tried not to fidget on my walk from my car to the restaurant but all I wanted to do was yank at my skirt to pull it down to its original location. It was still surprisingly windy outside and my hair was blowing in the wind, getting tossed in and out of my eyes in the process. I wasn't certain, but I said to myself, **Wow – I didn't know that Milestones had a doorman...? They've really taken things up a notch.**

The doorman turned out to be none other than Jake, looking handsome in a crisp navy suit. I had never seen him out of his hockey gear before and I guess my windblown hair skewed my usually-perfect vision. When I realized it was him opening the door for me, I couldn't help but laugh, all, while he greeted me with a kiss on each cheek. It was very French. Innocent yet intimate.

We both admitted to not being overly hungry, so we went for a bit of a light supper: a couple of appetizers with an entrée to share. And wine. Two big glasses of wine – one red; one white.

Sooooooo…! He said with enthusiasm; **How did it go? Tell me all about your big presentation today.**

I shared with him how I got out of my car, looking and feeling completely charged and confident to sell our big language proposal to the guy who controlled the purse strings. I had **I've got this!** written all over me. I was laughing and blushing at the same time as I told Jake how, as I was walking towards the conference centre, a huge gust of wind came out of nowhere, catching my skirt in the process. It wasn't just any skirt - it was the fullest wrap-skirt you can possibly imagine. The endless amount of fabric got swept up, literally reaching high above my head, giving me my very own unforgettable Marilyn Monroe moment. To top it all off, the sight of my black lace panties triggered an excited old man to stick his head out his car window and yell ***WAHOO!*** at the top of his lungs.

It was hilarious and humiliating, all in one, I admitted.

The conversation was easy, floating smoothly from one topic to the next. We laughed a lot. We shared food. We drank wine. We told secrets. He wanted to know about my other four dates – not in a jealous kind of way, but wanting in on the fun. He raised his eyebrows about the sexual planning from **Bachelor # 2** but then suggested that I could have sex with **Bachelor # 3** on those granite countertops that he could install for me.

We ordered another glass of wine between us. I reached for my old glass as the waiter was taking it away, but Jake let him go. We would share. I guess we *had* known each other for six months. It's not like we were strangers...

Like the day the dressing room had emptied out around us, so, too, had the restaurant tonight. I loved this feeling of being submersed in our own little world, completely oblivious to everything going on around us. It felt soothingly warm and natural.

As we wandered out of the restaurant, I couldn't help but hope he wouldn't see my fresh scar on the back of my leg as he walked behind me. But then I realized: Why should it really matter? It is, what it is. I got over it as quickly as it entered my mind.

He walked me to my car where the dialogue continued with a rare cocktail of nervousness and comfort. This was quickly cut short as he casually opened up my car door for me, and all I kept thinking was, **Gasp!!! Thank GOD I cleaned the inside of my car!** I would have died of embarrassment had the usual juice boxes and granola bars fallen out in a shameful display. It instantly made me think of my friends Carolyn and Terry on their wedding night in Montreal many years ago. The doorman of their luxury hotel opened up the door of their limo, only to have McDonald's cups and styrofoam containers fall all over his patent leather shoes. It was hilarious for them, swimming in champagne, but I don't think it would have the same effect on a first date like this.

Mission Accomplished

I snuck inside Julia's majestic front door and quietly tip-toed towards the wooden staircase. I grabbed the glass of wine that rested on the banister with the urgent message written on a yellow Post-it note: **HURRY! I'm upstairs!!** Never a night owl, but there's nothing like getting a story hot-off-the-press, and so there was no way that Julia was going to miss this post-game debrief. She deliberately left the house unlocked for me and forced herself to stay awake so we could have this premeditated minute-by-minute dissection of my evening. (~ It's a girl thing.)

I curled up on her enormous bed that was already starting to fill up. Julia was there, snuggled in with her laptop on her tummy and Grace was fast asleep beside her. I had seen Tim on my route to the master bedroom, passed out on top of Georgia's bed with a picture book fallen on top of his face. I knew we had plenty of time to ourselves before any one of them would come to.

I was surprisingly relaxed, almost limp, lacking all angst and buzz you typically feel after a first date. It was remarkably similar to the end of my university final exams. After four long years of endeavouring to get to the finish line of such an exceptional journey, it was all a bit anticlimactic.

The same was true for this night.

I had first met Jake in November, a long and full six months ago. Cameron and another player had been traded onto his hockey team partway into the season and they were having a team party, in part to welcome the two new boys, but also to build camaraderie amongst all of the players and parents.

When Cameron and I first walked into the party, I cringed from head to toe, furious with my bad luck. I spotted Bill over in the corner, the father of the worst bully in the league, and I was mortified that we were now stuck on the same team. So, you can imagine my shock and elation when that same father came up to me and said, **Hi. I'm Jake. I'll be coaching your son this season.** I've never been so happy to be so wrong. How is it that two unrelated men can look so much alike? Who cares! Relief never felt so good.

To steal a line from *Jerry McGuire*, he had me at hello. I was washed with an instant warm feeling all over, from the moment he shook my hand at the party. I can still remember the jeans and white cotton shirt he was wearing, imprinting an indelible visual image in my mind. He later gave an informal speech to the parents over drinks, as the boys played mini-sticks in the basement. Ahhh - a man who was handsome *and* had great leadership: I liked him from the get-go.

Time (and a bitterly cold winter) found me gradually thinking of him more and more outside of hockey. This was one of the good guys ~ a man I definitely wanted to explore and get to know better.

So, how did it go??? Julia begged.

It was...perfect, I said as I laid my head down on one of Tim's pillows, eyes closed with a deep smile consuming my face.

Really?

Best-date-ever.

So, did you kiss him? The date was your initiative, so I assume the kiss would come from you...?

No kiss. Eyes still closed. **I don't want to taste the wine if I can't drink it.**

By this point, Julia was completely lost, and, due to her sleepy state and desperation to get the details out of me urgently, she could not follow my metaphor to save her life.

Wait – best date of your life, no kiss and you didn't drink any wine??

By this point, Tim had joined us, leaving me the only one above the covers. Julia wanted him to throw in his two cents to give us a man's perspective. The fact that he had been following my journey from the beginning definitely made him qualified to participate.

He doesn't want to date her. Oh, trust me ~ he wants to hook up. Just not date her. Who knows what's going on behind the scenes in his life right now, messing things up, but now is not the right time for him. But, hey ~ that's just my take. What do I know?

Always incredibly succinct, Tim was probably right.

Jake is an amazing guy ~ I loved every moment together and every phone call over the past hockey season. I'd certainly be willing to go out with him again, but I had a pretty good hunch that it likely wasn't meant to be. Kate, my life coach friend, once gave me some free advice on the matter: a relationship needs to be an oasis ~ a true source of escape and joy. It shouldn't be a foundation of stress or angst, always wondering when he will call...if he will call.

Jake had been giving me vibes for 6 months – friendliness, at first, which grew into curiosity, which then developed into a definite attraction. It got to the point where I was sure I could feel it every time we were together. He would call me instead of just hitting the reply button on e-mails…pull me aside frequently to chat at the rink…invite me to help him out on the bench when the assistant coach was away.

He was clear with his good-bye to me at the year-end party and it felt like that was that. I then threw out a net to everyone I knew, including him, looking for the people in my world to play cupid for me. But he stepped up to be more than just a matchmaker ~ he threw himself right into the heart of the game.

He was the star player of my dating assignment, even upping the ante from coffee to drinks to dinner, enduring as the front-runner from start to finish.

Interested, obviously...yet, it took him four weeks to be able to fit me in. During phone conversations, he would reveal how, when he gets home from a long, hard day - or worse, from a business trip – he shuts down and blocks out the outside world, just wanting to be alone. Add the Wednesday night soccer and the Friday night men's hockey into the mix, plus having his son every weekend, and, really – where would I fit in? It's no wonder it took him a month to finally be able to commit to our date.

Maybe it was just a "right place at the wrong time" kind of thing with us. But Julia was correct a while ago ~ I had had some reservations about our compatibility as I was getting to know him over the winter, plus a promise to myself to start trusting my gut.

Tim was right. Buddies it would likely be. Time would tell ~

~

As promised, we had my fait accompli party at the end of it all, to celebrate my inexplicable bravery of executing my master man-plan. The top three bachelors were not invited, as **Bachelor # 2** had suggested with such confident optimism. It was just a beautiful bouquet of girlfriends getting together to drink some wine, to laugh at life and to be inspired by each other ~ easily, the best mentors and motivators that life has to offer.

And isn't that the foundation of a true Girlfriend Manifesto? To break bread together through thick and thin; to bring to the table authentic joy and heartfelt honesty; and to learn and draw inspiration from each other's celebrations and setbacks, with forward momentum being the end goal for each of us…for all of us.

This adventure of mine that we were celebrating was completely steered and propelled by the vibrant presence of my inner circle ~ an ensemble of strong, dynamic women whose camaraderie formed the emotional bedrock of my journey. Their wisdom, wit, and unwavering support repeatedly lifted me up and showed me that confidence arises from the strength of collective sisterhood. Because, when women link arms, magic happens. When girlfriends gather with intention, connection happens, trust happens… empowerment happens. We evolve. We blossom. We shine. We step into an entirely reimagined and redirected future when we are surrounded by friendship that feels like home.

And that is what was at the true heart of our tiny gala. As we raised our glasses of Moët in the glow of the candles, we celebrated what started as five playful dates but organically developed into a mindset and a movement of women who not only show up for themselves, but show up for each other, in every conceivable way…resulting in the kind of growth you just can't do alone.

.

Ripple Effect

Perhaps the most surprising and rewarding part of the whole adventure was delivered months later in a very unexpected message:

From: Charlotte
To: Sophie
Subject: Ripple effect
Date: Monday, August 10 8:20 pm

Hey Sophie,

What's up with the continuation of the coffee dates? More importantly, what's your next goal in life?

I was inspired by *your* goal-setting and entered a triathlon. Yes... goal-setters always inspire me. Sometimes it even "takes" and I do something. In your case, it worked! I am thankful for the confluence of good girlfriends and good timing!

It went so well that I have entered another one with really significant distances (750 m swim...30 km bike...7 km run). This is a major stretch for me but I now know I can do it, and my last month of training involves doing things to improve my finish-time.

I'm having a blast and even enjoying the workouts!

So, Sophie, the moral of the story is...you shouldn't be surprised if you flutter your butterfly wings and then learn that someone else was inspired to take flight with their own exciting, life-altering dreams :)

Take care.

Charlotte

P.S. Goals involving men are complicated! Goals involving swim-bike-run are so much easier ;)

The End

(Sort of...)

The Academics of It All...

I guess, in hindsight, the purpose of the **5 Dates** Man-Plan was not just to find Mr. Right, after all. It was more to get me back in the game; to coach me…to nudge me back in the direction of feeling comfortable again at the sound of those two little words: first date. Each word stands alone as quite ordinary, but, when combined, become enormously threatening yet promising… terrifying yet enticing and potentially lovely.

The biggest aha moment for me was the realization that, just because two people don't end up together, at the end of a date or at the end of a lifetime, doesn't mean that one was not *good enough* for the other or that one was *better* than the other. Bottom line ~ it doesn't mean rejection, or superior vs. inferior. Those words should be completely stripped from the whole language of relationships. When two people don't end up together, it is often a case of one of them realizing the hard truth and sad reality that the two of them are not properly matched. They just figure it out sooner, find the courage to admit it sooner…and finally let go sooner than the other person.

Dating, mating, matchmaking – whatever you want to call it – it's all about the right fit, more than how perfect two people are together on paper. It always amazes me how so many tend to think that two nice people should stay together, or how the world is shocked when an aesthetically gorgeous couple does not last 'til death do them part. You love who you love. You don't love who you don't love…regardless of what the outside world expects or what an algorithm determines. And, apparently, the scientific and anthropological research shows that there is no magic formula to predict or explain our choices for falling in - or out - of love.

When the day came, having to sit down with my 5-year-old son to tell him that Mommy and Daddy would not be living together anymore, I pulled out a puzzle and spread it out across the dining room table. His dad, sitting right next to me, was kind, loving, thoughtful. Perfect for me in my twenties…just not the right match for me in the end, long-term. Life changes. People change...in ways that they, themselves, can never predict, such that the "right match" then becomes "once a right match".

We nervously procrastinated the inevitable, but I finally found the strength to say the words that I never expected Cameron to hear at any point in his lifetime. I prefaced the discussion with a talk about puzzles; about how families are like puzzles. The Mommy and Cameron pieces always fit together and the Daddy and Cameron pieces always fit together. But sometimes the Mommy and Daddy pieces don't always fit together. You try really, really hard to put them together, but sometimes they just won't fit.

And as juvenile as it may sound, the same is true in the world of dating. Just because I didn't continue dating those men doesn't make me any better than them. In fact, the five bachelors were each superior to me in one way or another: one was more intellectual, one was much more entertaining, one was more talented, another more financially successful and yet another, maybe a few of those traits combined. Bachelors 1 through 5 were great men ~ *really* great men. They just were not the right fit for me. Nor I for them. And that's OK.

For myself, I have finally figured out that the right person for me isn't necessarily someone who meets the criteria of a lengthy checklist of physical and personality traits. A man who is visual perfection, with Hollywood looks and a perfect body, might get a second look from me but has to linger in just the right wavelength and energy zone to sustain my interest. I have dated the best-looking man in the room, the smartest, the nicest, the most talented and I've dated the richest man in the room, over the course of my lifetime. But I now realize that the right man for me is not someone who scores the best in every category, but, rather, is someone who makes me like myself the best when I am with him…someone who brings out my favourite sides of my own personality when we are texting, talking or touching. That is the exclusive key that opens my heart ~ the secret recipe for a lengthy, sustainable match made in heaven for me, inside and out.

What this **5 Dates** dating project did for me – this wacky amalgamation of blind dating...meets internet dating...meets The Bachelorette – was give me, by far, the best ego boost of my life, and the very best girlfriend camaraderie experience I could have ever wished for.

For weeks and weeks, I was revered as a courageous, sizzling superstar in ways I never could have predicted. By setting and publicly striving towards a very personal goal ~ by saying my hopes and dreams out loud to the people in my universe, I became an anomaly that sparked intense curiosity. I was doing something that some really brave and really accomplished people told me they could never do. And because of that, people sat up and listened. "My people" watched me declare that I wanted more out of life, and they watched, with amazement – maybe with a little shock and awe, and maybe, in some cases, with a bit of envy – the steps that I took to climb my way through this journey, one stride at a time, one bachelor at a time.

What makes us uniquely human is the true desire for those immediately around us - those in our individual villages - to be happy and successful. Sure, there is the whole survival of the fittest thing that makes things a little messy sometimes. But, when that gets pushed out of the way, life is very sweet; people are very sweet. My network not only wanted to know every detail of my quest, they wanted to actively participate in me reaching my goal by providing me with bachelors, dating attire and, best of all, advice and encouragement. They truly, truly wanted me to thrive and reach my target.

What's the saying? Misery enjoys company? So, too, does happiness.

I proved that it takes a village, not only to raise a child in this world, but, also, to direct each of us towards our best life; to push us towards reaching our fullest potential. Not that having a man in my life is the realization of my fullest potential ~ it's just something that I am ready for right now, at this stage in my life. And, it's the journey that I selected that took a village. *My* village. A big hamlet full of cupids and an award-worthy supporting cast.

I began my **5 Dates** journey feeling very reluctant – *hugely* reluctant - as a result of having struggled through a difficult and taxing relationship. Despite the passage of time, it is a memory that fades far too slowly. And as a result, I was timid and unsure and anxious about diving into the world of dating again, as evidenced by nearly passing out while announcing my mission to my entire social network.

It felt like the biggest risk of my life, but in hindsight, there was nothing risky about it at all. There was no danger. No threat. Nothing was at stake. Nothing was in jeopardy.

The reality is that only good things emerged from this wacky and wonderful social experiment. I grew and I matured. My grey matter expanded. I'm sure of it. And I became so confident in who I am that I became fearless. Fearless of the process. Fearless of looking vulnerable. Fearless of the unknown.

What Now?
Moving Forward

1) **Everyone loves a beautiful dream. Bring others into yours.**

How? Say your dreams out loud to people ~ even to total strangers, if you can slip it into the conversation somehow. Join the movement to **use your own personal network** to help you activate and achieve your goals in life. Whether your goal is to start dating again, enter a triathlon, quit smoking, create a garden, sell your house or move to the other side of the world...**go get it. Go out and do it.** Grab the bull by the horns, announce your goal to your network, get them involved, and see where the universe takes you.

You'll be surprised by how easy it really is to follow through with the steps that could change your world in the most unpredictable ways. And why wouldn't you jump at an opportunity that could stack the odds in your favour of making amazing, positive changes in your life?

My dating project somehow took a turn that inspired me to write a novel and create **the app 5 Dates Plan** for people who want to create their own dating adventure. That was never, ever part of the original plan in any shape or form, yet it has created an extraordinary journey that has completely redirected my life in ways that I never could have imagined.

2) **Start trusting your instincts** in the way that they were intended to be used.

3) **Raise and tweak your personal standards for the men and women that you allow in your life.** Who in your life follows the ideals of your girlfriend manifesto? Or, perhaps more importantly, who in your life does not?

4) **Find the strength,** with the help of your own inner voice and your tight circle of friends, **to break the addiction** that comes with love or lust, when it really is time to let go.

Instead of it being 'easier said than done', leaving a wrong relationship was 'easier done than said' for me – the anticipation truly was the very worst part, in my case. When I finally took action, the relief was incredible.

I once told a friend that, if you are finding it impossible to leave a relationship yet desperately want to, be inspired by the billions of people who were once in your shoes, who then ended up in my shoes. You, too, can get there.

If and when you do get to the other side, you will look at those around you and realize who should end their mismatched relationships. You will know the feeling of 'before leaving' and 'after leaving' and wish those people around you could find the courage to walk away, as well.

Nina Simone got it right: **"You've got to learn to leave the table when love is no longer being served."**

5) **Be relieved of any guilt** you may have for ending a marriage or relationship that needed ending.

6) **Be inspired to be yourself.** Skip the constant make-up, the fake

nails, the hair extensions. At least give it a try ~ start small by scaling back, bit by bit, and let your natural beauty shine.

7) **Express yourself.** Live without regrets.

Consider telling that secret someone about your affections for them, even if it is shared on the smallest scale. At least, if it doesn't lead anywhere, you won't spend the rest of your life agonizing over should have/would have/could have...forever wondering, forever grieving over a life that never happened.

You might just find out that he or she really wasn't actually right for you. And better to find out sooner, than never knowing at all.

Imagine the potential happiness you may miss out on, just because you sat at home longing for someone who wasn't the perfect fit that you thought they were. **Better to know than to waste precious time on a very wrong, very inaccurate fairy tale.**

8) But, above all else, remember to **aim high.**

A lifetime is a very long time to be locked inside the same body, with the same voice yattering away in your head at you, wishing you had done this or that, or longing for a shift in your life's journey.

If you really want your dream to happen, then stick with it. Not for the money or the fame, but because it makes your heart and soul sing.

Don't let fear be your barrier to the changes you long for. Push that send button. It's not as hard as you think. And the results will truly amaze you.

Notable Quotes From Within (A Cheat-Sheet For Life & Love)

Love Addiction

When we are addicted to alcohol, drugs, gambling…we betray our loved ones. But, when we are addicted to love, we betray ourselves.

My heart had previously been guilty of getting drunk with lust and infatuation too quickly, smudging my vision of reality.

Experience has taught me the hard way that being alone is a lot less lonely than being in a relationship full of chaos and drama.

Bottom line: love shouldn't be this hard. You shouldn't have to go to the ends of the earth, just to try to survive – literally or figuratively – within the confines of a relationship.

"You've got to learn to leave the table when love is no longer being served." **Nina Simone**

"A real man will ruin your lipstick…not your mascara." **Unknown**

Instincts

I always thought that it was just an expression. But those fine little hairs that you can barely see back there [on the back of your neck]? They really do stand straight up. Like a highly trained soldier. It is your body telling you, **I can't explain this in 3 seconds or less, but you need to turn around and run like hell.** Which we never do. And by we, I mean women. We likely have the strongest instincts on the planet, yet for some unknown reason, we seem to trust ourselves the least in this world. It really is like having your very best friend propped up high on your left shoulder, looking out for you from every angle. And why wouldn't we trust our very best friend???

It's like each warning signal my body sent me was snuffed out as quickly and as easily as the flame of a candle. With one fell swoop, extinguished…dismissed. I'd been treating my instincts throughout my life as if they were more of a malfunction rather than the survival tool that they truly are.

My next New Year's Resolution? Know when to walk away from a train wreck.

It took a lot less energy to actually go with my gut instead of fighting against it, as I had too many times before in my life. Note to self: Oprah was right – trust my gut.

A Healthy Happiness

"As I see it, a family that split up was not a family that failed in this case – just a family that was led by adults who saw a better path." **Charlotte**

"Don't be perfect – just be yourself." **Goldie Hawn** quoting her mother's life lesson on Oprah's Master Class.

What's the saying? Misery enjoys company? So, too, does happiness.

I'm not looking for someone to go out with. I just want to find a man to stay home with.

It seems that people just can't get enough of this concept of putting a goal out there and actively getting your entire support network to help you reach that goal. It's like everyone has intuitively made it their personal responsibility to catapult me across the finish line.

"Love is everything it's cracked up to be. It really is worth fighting for, being brave for, risking everything for. And the trouble is, if you don't risk anything, you risk even more." Erica Jong

I now realize that the right man for me is not someone who scores the best in every category, but, rather, is someone who makes me like myself the best when I am with him…someone who brings out my favourite sides of my own personality when we are texting, talking or touching.

~

...But, perhaps the most relevant quote of all comes from the brilliant and insightful Orson Welles himself:

If you want a happy ending,

that depends, of course, on where you stop your story.

So…go. Be happy. Be kind. Help others. Reach out when you need assistance. Use your network. Trust your instincts. Make life choices that are best for your heart & soul…best for your health & happiness. Be brave. You'll recover if it doesn't work out as planned. But show up and try. Try hard. Chase your dreams, whatever they may be. Remember what Jonathan

Winters said: If your ship doesn't come in, swim out to meet it. If your hopes and dreams don't come to you, go get them. Make them happen. Look around ~ find your role models ~ and be inspired by those people who went after *their* dreams. You'll realize that you, too, can do the very same, in your own unique way. Whether it be love, adventure or laughter…go fix that broken spoke in your Wheel of Life. Take control ~ be the CEO of your own life's journey. And have a spectacular time discovering what life really does have to offer.

By the way ~ what *are* your hopes and dreams?

Susie Ashmore

xoxox

Thank You for Reading! 💕
Did *The Girlfriend Manifesto* make you smile, reflect, or feel inspired in any way?

If so, I'd love it if you could write a quick review on Amazon ~ just a line or two would be perfect!
Your words help other readers find the book, which could have a big impact on someone's life.

With gratitude,
Susie x

See below for details of Susie's

Collective Sparkle Workshop.